THEIR HIGHLAND BEGINNING

THE CLAN SINCLAIR BOOK SIX

CELESTE BARCLAY

OLIVER HEBER BOOKS

All rights reserved.

No part of this publication may be sold, copied, distributed, reproduced or transmitted in any form or by any means, mechanical or digital, including photocopying and recording or by any information storage and retrieval system without the prior written permission of both the publisher, Oliver Heber Books and the author, Celeste Barclay, except in the case of brief quotations embodied in critical articles and reviews.

PUBLISHER'S NOTE: This is a work of fiction. Names, characters, places, and incidents either are the product of the author's imagination or are used fictitiously. Any resemblance to actual persons, living or dead, business establishments, events, or locales is entirely coincidental.

Copyright © 2018 by Celeste Barclay.

0 9 8 7 6 5 4 3 2 1

Published by Oliver Heber Books

❦ Created with Vellum

This book is dedicated to all the authors who have helped guide me through the process of becoming a published author. Without their knowledge and experience, I would not have written this prequel or been so successful.

Thank you

Happy reading, y'all.

SUBSCRIBE TO CELESTE'S NEWSLETTER

Subscribe to Celeste's bimonthly newsletter to receive exclusive insider perks.

Have you read *Their Highland Beginning, The Clan Sinclair Prequel?* Learn how the saga begins! This FREE novella is available to all new subscribers to Celeste's monthly newsletter. Subscribe on her website.

Subscribe Now

THE CLAN SINCLAIR

Book 1 *His Highland Lass*
   Mairghread Sinclair and Tristan Mackay

Book 2 *His Bonnie Highland Temptation*
   Callum Sinclair and Siùsan Mackenzie

Book 3 *His Highland Prize*
   Alexander Sinclair and Brighde Kerr

Book 4 *His Highland Pledge*
   Magnus Sinclair and Deirdre Fraser

Book 5 *His Highland Surprise*
   Tavish Sinclair and Ceit Comyn

Book 6 *Their Highland Beginning*
   Liam Sinclair and Kyla Sutherland

SINCLAIR FAMILY TREE

Liam Sinclair m. Kyla Sutherland

b. Callum Sinclair m. Siùsan Mackenzie (SH-IY-oo-san)
    b. Thormud Seamus Magnus Sinclair (TOR-mood SHAY-mus)
    b. Rose Kyla Sinclair

b. Alexander Sinclair m. Brighde Kerr (BREE-ju KAIR)

b. Tavish Sinclair m. Ceit Comyn (KAIT-ch CUM-in)

b. Magnus Sinclair m. Deidre Fraser (DEER-dreh FRA-zer)

b. Mairghread Sinclair m. Tristan Mackay (Mah-GAID)
    b. "Wee" Liam Brodie Mackay

FOREWORD

The Clan Sinclair is an actual clan from the very northern reaches of Scotland near the Orkney Islands. They have existed in that area for centuries making the most out of the land and sea. The novels that are The Clan Sinclair are purely works of fiction. Some names may be similar or same to actual men and women who lived during the time of my novels, but that is purely coincidence. I have taken quite a bit of creative license to conjure up plots that I hope you enjoy.

While historians have shown that plaids worn as kilts did not occur until roughly the 1700s, I like a man in a kilt, and I thought you might too. So, while this is a medieval series, I took more creative license here too.

This prequel introduces you to the patriarch and matriarch of this generation's Clan Sinclair. This is a novella that is set before the five main novels of the series. Perhaps it will answer any questions you might have after reading the other books in the series, or perhaps it will inspire you to read about the five Sinclair siblings and their fated loves.

Meet the members of Clan Sinclair in this five book Highland romance series. The Clan Sinclair features Mairghread and her four brothers, Callum, Alexander, Tavish, and

Magnus. Each member of the Scottish clan faces challenges as they meet their fated match, but all the Sinclairs find their HEA. Each novel in the series is a standalone, but they are best read together.

I hope you enjoy.

PROLOGUE

Laird Liam Sinclair sat before the roaring fire in the Great Hall listening to his children chatter. His four sons and one daughter were adults now, and he had a more extended family than he could have wished for.

The chatter and banter, along with the wails and squeals from a few babes, drifted to the back of his mind as he thought of his deceased wife.

Bonnie Kyla, if only ye could be here to see how our children have grown. Ye'd be mighty proud of them, but I suppose ye are watching and guiding them. I believe we've received more than one divine intervention, and I've felt yer hand in all of them. How I miss everything about ye. Hagatha keeps the fresh flowers in the chamber ye and I shared for too short a time. The scent of lemongrass will most likely always be there. If nae from a vase, then in ma memory and ma heart. The chamber seems so large now for only me. It's been a lonely life without ye even with our children. I ken ye told me to move on, but I couldnae and canna stomach the idea of someone other than ye, mo chridhe. There's never been anyone else since that first day in the Great Hall. Do ye remember, mo ghaol?

CHAPTER ONE

"Da, it's nae too late to call this off. I dinna have to marry some Sutherland chit to end the feud. We cede them that rocky patch near the border Grandfather won from the Gunns. They gain the plot, and we call it a day. Or better yet, we call Dugan home from fostering, and ma baby brother can marry her."

"Ye ken the contracts have been signed by both me and the lass's father. Laird Sutherland wouldnae stand for ye setting her aside, and I willna either. I dinna understand yer objection. Ye're of an age to wed, and ye must have heirs the same as I did. She may vera well surprise ye. Yer mother did."

"Ye and Mama were a love match. It wasna a surprise to anyone when ye wed. Or that I arrived nearly nine moons later to the day."

"Dinna be cheeky. Ye're nae too old or too big for me to skelp yer arse. "

That should have been enough of a warning for Liam Sinclair, heir to his father, Laird Donnell Sinclair. But on this day, he had his dander up. His father announced his betrothal a moon ago, and the woman was set to arrive at any minute.

"How old is she anyway?"

"She's close in age to yer score and four summers. She's a score and two."

"More than a score and she isnae wed yet? What's wrong with her? Does she have warts and claws? Mayhap missing a few teeth? She certainly sounds a bit long in the tooth. Da, look at me. I am vera serious. Mayhap she--"

A very soft and a very decidedly feminine clearing of the throat came from behind him. Liam froze before taking a deep breath and turning around. The sight that greeted him made the air whoosh from him, and he felt as if he had been pole-axed in the gut. The woman who stood before him was more than bonnie, she was beautiful. Liam took in the jet-black hair and bright lapis lazuli blue eyes. There was a faint dimple in her left cheek, and her eyebrows looked like they were sketched in by a master artisan. Her nose was short and soft at the end. She was not very tall, and Liam was sure she would barely come to the center of his chest when he held her.

Hold her. Where the bluidy hell did that come from? A moment ago, I was ready to flee into the hills and live the life of a hermit.

Liam noticed her ample curves. She was slightly broader in the hips than was considered the standard among noble women, but Liam found he rather liked the fact that while petite, she looked sturdy. At only four and twenty, he was already a large man standing at nearly six and a half feet. He knew his shoulders had not stopped broadening even though he had to nearly turn sideways to pass through many doorways.

"Shut yer gob, son. Ye're catching flies," came the none too quiet whisper from behind. Liam could hear the laughter in his father's voice, but it did not bother him.

He reached out his hand, and when she placed her tiny one above it, he bowed and kissed the back of her hand. He felt more than heard the tiny gasp when his lips actually pressed against her satiny skin. Liam did register her palms and fingertips were rough and calloused, but he was at least well-mannered enough not to bring his observation to anyone's notice.

"Lady Kyla, welcome to Castle Dunbeath." Liam could not think of anything more to say without it sounding like a lie after being caught saying such unfavorable things.

"Thank ye, Lord Liam. I see ye are a giant as I was told, but ye dinna seem quite as fierce as I was warned. More like a deerhound than a bear," she said in the demurest voice she could muster.

Liam stood wide-eyed for a moment as her comment fully sunk in. As a warrior and as heir to a clan as large as the Sinclairs, his reputation and the safety of his clan depended upon his being fierce. However, the politely stated insult was precisely what he deserved, and he knew it. Liam tilted his head back and roared with laughter before looking down at his very bonnie and very spunky bride.

Bride. I'm already thinking of her as such. Ma goose is cooked.

"Lord Liam," Lady Kyla loudly whispered, "I dinna think ye should laugh quite so much. Ye sound like a stuck bore. Ye may have the healer called."

That only made him laugh all the harder. When he looked down at her as he finally caught his breath, he saw her sly grin.

"Ye have pluck. I'll give ye that. Ye will fit in vera well here, and I deserved that in spades." Liam became serious as he gazed into the depths of her blue eyes. "Ye dinna deserve to be insulted in such a way whether ye were present to hear it or nae. Ma foul temper shouldnae hurt ye. I'm vera sorry, ma lady."

Kyla's eyes opened wide for only a passing moment before she cocked her head slightly and nodded.

"Thank ye for yer apology. It is appreciated and accepted."

Kyla looked beyond Liam's shoulder to see a bear of a man who was almost identical to Liam except for having grey hair instead of a rich chestnut like Liam's. An elegant woman came to join them, and Liam's father wrapped his arm around her waist, pulling her to his side. Kyla immediately recognized them to be Liam's parents, Laird Donnell and Lady Arabella Sinclair.

She bowed her head and dropped into a graceful curtsy before her soon-to-be parents by marriage. She kept her head down as was expected until she was acknowledged. She was not anticipating the large but gentle hand that was placed slightly behind her elbow or the soft pull that brought her upright. Her eyes flew to the man standing next to her. Kyla could not help but stare into eyes so brown they looked like barrel-aged whisky. It was like the world floated away from her at that moment. She had moments ago been insulted and teased by this very man, but something in the way he touched her suddenly made her keenly aware of his masculinity and virility. Liam Sinclair was the singularly most handsome man she had ever seen. She swallowed twice before she looked back at Laird and Lady Sinclair.

Lady Sinclair had stepped forward, and Kyla had not even noticed. Her cheeks pinkened as she realized this very elegant lady caught Kyla staring at her very handsome son.

"Welcome to Castle Dunbeath, Lady Kyla. I hope ye will feel welcome here, and I look forward to getting to ken ye better." Kyla, nor Liam, missed Lady Arabella's pointed comment about feeling welcome in the future as opposed to right now. Kyla nearly bit her lower lip, a nervous habit she had been trying to break herself of for years, but she thought better of it. She could see Liam with her peripheral vision and was overly aware of his physical presence as he still held her arm.

"Ye are vera kind, Lady Sinclair. I do feel welcome already. It is quite like being home with ma brothers. They tease me often and mercilessly." As soon as she finished speaking, she wanted to cringe. Liam dropped his hand the moment she compared him to her brothers. No bridegroom wanted to be told his bride considered him as more of a brother than a husband. She turned her head to look at Liam. "I mean to say a little goading feels familiar and makes arriving here a little less daunting."

Liam offered her a tight smile. Kyla wanted to sink into the floor. While he failed to make a good first impression with her, she was now failing miserably in front of his parents, the leaders of the entire clan. She knew word of their conversation would soon be buzzing about the keep, if not the village she passed through on her arrival.

Lady Arabella stepped further forward and took both of Kyla's hands in hers. Kyla immediately noticed how soft and smooth Lady Arabella's hands were compared to hers. She wanted to pull them away and hide them in her skirts, but she knew that would make her even more conspicuous.

"First of all, ma dear, I amnae Lady Sinclair to anyone here. I am Lady Arabella, and since ye are to join ma family, I am simply Arabella to ye. Secondly, dinna fash over making a good impression. Ye already have. I heard what ye said to him, and ye putting him in his place every now and again willna hurt him. It might even make him a better mon." She grinned at her son as she waggled her eyebrows at him.

Kyla was charmed immediately with Arabella's kindness, and she suddenly became aware of an overwhelming desire to get to know her future mother-by-marriage better. She had been without a mother for so long she almost forgot what it was like to be cared for by an older matron. Arabella squeezed her hands before letting them go. Kyla felt like all the warmth surrounding her suddenly drained away. She looked over at Liam again who watched his mother. He turned to look at her, and once again, she felt like she was drowning in his enigmatic eyes. She could not read the look, and it made her feel shy and out of place after having been greeted so welcomingly.

"Lass, didna yer father accompany ye? I ken the documents have already been signed, but I would have thought he would come too."

Laird Sinclair looked directly at her, and she tried not to

shrink away. She returned his gaze, but before she could answer, she felt more than saw Liam's body shift towards her almost as though he was ready to protect her.

"Ma father was unable to escort me because of a raid on one of the villages just over a fortnight ago. It would seem we struggle to get along with our neighbors, the Rosses, too." Kyla held her chin up and would not cower before this mountain of a man. She saw and heard his good-natured comments to his son, but she was not entirely sure if he would welcome her as warmly now he knew her father opted not to accompany her. She looked over her shoulder and searched the people within the Great Hall.

"Ma uncle accompanied me, but I dinna seem to see him yet. He may still be in the bailey making arrangements for our guardsmen and the horses."

Kyla knew it was a weak excuse especially once they met him. More than likely, her uncle was already at the village tavern with a pint in one hand and a wench in the other. She tried not to grimace when she thought of him and how he behaved in front of her during their journey. She thanked all the angels and archangels that she was his niece, and therefore, held no interest to him.

"I amnae worried. I'm sure he will join us in time for the evening meal. I ken ye've had a long journey, lass, so would ye care to rest? Arabella has prepared a chamber for ye on the third floor. It's directly above the family chambers." Laird Donnell smiled kindly at her, and she realized he was rather fatherly despite being a renowned warrior.

Mayhap the apple didna fall far from the tree. Mayhap father and son live up to their fierce reputations, but they both seem less intimidating than I expected.

"Laird Sinclair, if ye dinna mind, I would like to stretch ma legs for a bit. I have been sitting for several days, and while a soft bed is appealing after the hard ground for so many nights, I really would like to move aboot a bit."

"It's Donnell, lass," he looked over at his wife who nodded

her head, "I'm sure Arabella would be happy to take ye to the Lady's garden."

Before Arabella or Kyla could answer, Liam stepped forward and placed Kyla's hand on his forearm.

"Da, ye ken Mama has many responsibilities as chatelaine at this time of day. I can show Lady Kyla to the garden," He looked down at Kyla and smiled, "and if she would like to, I can show her aboot the bailey too."

Why does he seem shy of a sudden? Does he think I could possibly decline in front of his parents?

"That sounds like a fine idea, lad." Donnell nodded to his son and then smiled down at Kyla. "Dinna hesitate to ask for aught ye need or want. This is yer home now."

Kyla knew this was her new home, and she even liked it from what she saw, but to hear it spoken aloud was rather jarring. All she could do was smile in return.

"Come, lass," Liam whispered in her ear.

CHAPTER TWO

Liam and Kyla made their way out the enormous double doors that led to the bailey. Kyla marveled at how wide they were but figured if all the Sinclair men were as wide and tall as the laird and his son, it was no small wonder they needed such massive doors. They were studded with metal rivets to reinforce them in case of attack, and a giant metal ring served as the handle. As they reached the steps leading to the ground, Liam covered the hand resting on his arm with his.

"They're a might steep if ye arenae used to them," Liam said by way of explanation for an action that might otherwise have been considered very forward. They might be betrothed, but they met only moments ago, and they were in public.

"Thank ye," Kyla said as she lifted her skirts to keep from tripping. The steps were quite steep.

They walked in silence until they reached the gate to a large garden. Kyla could see this was the plot that helped feed the entire keep. There were various vegetables and herbs growing in tidy lines. She looked around and felt excited at the prospect of spending time planting, weeding, and harvesting from the spacious area.

"Ye enjoy gardening." It was more of a statement than a question.

"Aye. How'd ye ken?"

"Yer eyes lit up when ye saw the plants, and I noticed yer hands are a bit rough. Dinna ye wear gloves?"

Kyla was not prepared to offer an explanation. She was not entirely sure she could trust Liam yet. He had been charming, once he knew she was there, and she was most assuredly very attracted to him, but his unkind words still lingered in the back of her mind.

"Nae always," was all she offered.

She watched as her brief answer sunk in. She was relieved when Liam only nodded and pointed towards a smaller gate at the far end of the keep's garden. When they arrived at it, he unlatched it and held it open. Kyla could not help her gasp as she stepped through into an oasis of flowers, blooming bushes, and trees laden with fruit.

"Do ye like it?"

Kyla jumped. She had not realized Liam stood so close that his warm breath brushed against her neck and ear.

"I didna mean to startle ye, Kyla. May I call ye that or do yer prefer Lady Kyla?"

"Ye didna startle me. I was a mite surprised to see such a beautiful garden tucked away in the corner." She was not about to admit how his presence affected her. "And I dinna mind Kyla, Liam."

She looked back over her shoulder and was about to cock an eyebrow when she came nearly nose to nose with Liam.

"I like to hear ma name come from ye." He said softly. They stood for a long moment gazing at one another. Kyla felt her mouth go dry, and she could not think of anything to say. She wondered if Liam might try to kiss her, they were standing so close.

Dear God, dinna let me make a fool of maself any more than I already have. I canna believe how petulant I sounded. I was being petulant. I hope Kyla doesnae thinks I'm spoiled, or worse cruel. I canna believe how beautiful she is. I can smell the scent of lemongrass when I stand this close. She's been traveling for days, and still smells like freshly cut flowers. I ken I should move away, but I dinna think I can. St Columba's bones, she has the reddest, fullest lips I have ever seen. I wonder how she tastes. What I wouldnae give for just a wee taste. Bluidy hell, Liam! Ye canna be kissing her in yer mother's garden within an hour of meeting her. Ye are an arse.

Liam reined in his racing thoughts and the temptation coursing through him and stepped around Kyla. He extended his arm to gesture she precede him. He was trying to be gallant, but he worried his gesture came across as ungracious, almost as if he were shooing her along.

"Ye can look around, Lady, I mean Kyla."

Ye are mucking this up. This is a right mess. Ye'll be lucky if she is even talking to ye by the evening meal. Ye are twice, nay thrice, an arse.

Kyla looked around for a moment and made her way to the corner farthest from the keep and the gate. She spotted a patch of lemongrass that was her favorite.

When she reached the stalks, she leaned over to take a sniff. Liam felt his cock harden at the sight of her round buttocks in the air. He fisted his hands to keep from reaching for her. He could not stop his mind from picturing what it would feel like to take her from behind. He shook his head to try to dislodge the image. He turned his attention back to what she was saying. He was in time to notice she saw him shaking his head.

Oh no. What is she saying? She's looking at me as if I've insulted her again.

"—the lemongrass if I canna have any. I'm sure I can make ma soap from something else."

Christ on the cross! She thinks I've just refused her the use of the lemongrass.

"Nay, it wasna that. I thought a fly landed on ma hair. Of course, ye can have as much lemongrass as ye would like. Ye make yer own soap?" The words spilled out of his mouth as he tried to steer them in a safer direction.

"Aye. I've made ma own soap for years. Ever since ma mother passed away."

"Do ye make anything else?"

"I make the candles, both tallow and beeswax, and I sew, as ye would expect," Kyla bristled.

Liam reached out and took her hands into his larger ones.

"Kyla, I dinna expect aught from ye. I'm confident ye are more than capable of running a household such as ours, but I dinna want ye to work because ye feel obligated. Ye dinna owe me, or this clan, aught. Ye will one day, God willing, be the Lady Sinclair. That comes with more than enough responsibility. I want ye to only do the work ye enjoy nae be a servant." He turned her hands over and ran his thumb over her palms. He lifted her palms to his mouth and brushed soft kisses across where her fingers met her palms and then each fingertip before kissing her palms.

"Kyla, how did yer hands get this way? This is more than only gardening or making candles and soap?" Liam asked softly.

Kyla felt a lump rise in her throat and tears pricked at the back of her eyelids. When she looked at Liam, she saw a man who cared enough to ask and not demand. She was not sure she could speak let alone tell him the truth.

"I often help around the keep. Ma mother passed away several years ago, and I have been chatelaine since then. There is much to be done in a keep that large. I help where it is needed."

Liam nodded his head, and Kyla thought her answer had been enough.

"Do ye ken I have met yer brothers several times? And a few of those times two were with their wives."

Christ on the cross! How am I going to get around this? It doesnae take much to understand what he's nae saying. Come up with something, Kyla!

"Lass, I amnae asking ye to tell me aught ye dinna want me to ken. Just ken I may figure it out on ma own. Ye may want to decide whether I learn yer version first or the one someone else tells me, or I come up with on ma own."

Liam let the matter rest when he let go of her hands and turned towards the lemongrass. He pulled a dirk from his belt and cut several shoots which he handed to her.

"Ye never need to ask if ye may have some. It is as much yers now as it is ma mama's." He walked a few steps away before cutting a small bouquet of violets, lavender, and roses. He inspected each rose stem and cut away all the thorns before handing the flowers to her.

"Would ye like me to show ye around the rest of the bailey? Or do ye wish to stay here a little longer? Is there aught else ye wish to do?"

Kyla sniffed her bouquet of flowers before she stood on her tiptoes. She could only barely reach Liam's chin, so she waggled her finger to indicate she wanted him to come closer. When she could reach his cheek, she pressed a soft kiss to his warm and slightly prickly skin.

"Thank ye, Liam." Liam understood she referred to more than the flowers.

"Always, Kyla."

The two spent nearly an hour more in the garden as she explained various flowers and their medicinal powers. Liam never paid much attention to such things even when his mother tried to explain them. Kyla pointed out one day he and his men might be in a battle too far away for a healer to reach them in time. A little knowledge about local flora might save his life. Liam was forced to admit that situation already arose more than once in his young life.

Once they toured the Lady's garden, they crossed back into the larger vegetable and herb garden. They paused there to watch as several women tended the soil. Kyla pointed out more herbs and even some vegetables that could be used to cure illnesses and ailments. Liam was surprised at her vast knowledge. He wanted to ask where she learned so much, but he did not want to press her for any more information than she was willing to volunteer.

After they left the gardens, Liam showed her the various storerooms, the smithy, the distillery, and vintner's sheds, and he pointed out the postern gate. As they passed the laundresses, Kyla paused. Liam noticed she often started to bite her lower lip but stopped before doing it.

"Lass, what is the matter? Ye're trying nae to bite yer lip again. Something is bothering ye."

Kyla's eyes widened when she realized he already picked up on a habit she spent years unsuccessfully trying to break, and he understood when she did it.

"It's naught really. I just---Nay, it's nae important."

"Dinna fib, lass. If something is bothering ye, I dinna want ye to feel like ye canna tell me. Kyla, I dinna want a marriage with lies and secrets, so beginning our betrothal with any isnae a good start."

Kyla could feel the heat rising in her cheeks. She could barely remember what made her pause to begin with. Now she felt her temper flare at Liam's highhandedness. She grabbed the corner of his sleeve and tugged him out of earshot of those around them. Once she checked no one was watching them, she poked her finger into his chest.

"Dinna call me a liar. I may be quite a few things, but I dinna lie. I was concerned aboot the laundresses' use of lye soap that hasnae any herbs steeped in warm water first. I can smell the difference. It isnae any great catastrophe, but over time, the raw lye soap will wear away the material faster than it should. It could cause holes or the material to weaken and rip. I wasna going to say aught now because ye arenae yer mother, ye arenae a laundress, and I didna think ye'd be interested in how yer leines are washed as long as they show up clean in yer chest. I was going to speak to yer mother at a more convenient time. But, nay, ye couldnae let sleeping dogs lie. Ye tell me ye dinna want secrets or lies between us. Well, I'll tell ye I dinna want false accusations or needless suspicion in ma marriage, so it better nae begin with our betrothal. Ma thoughts are ma own until *I* decide to share them."

By this point, Kyla's face turned almost a shade of plum, her finger quivered as she continued to poke it into Liam's chest, and she was out of breath when she finished. Liam had never seen a more glorious sight in all his life.

"Ye're right, and I'm sorry."

Before she could respond, he leaned forward and kissed her. When she did not push him away, he slowly wrapped his arms around her waist and drew her to him. She knew she could not possibly reach his neck, so she settled for fisting her hands into his leine. The kiss was tender and inquisitive. Liam did not try to force more upon her, and he could tell she was very inexperienced. He slid his tongue along the seam of her lips but did not press for more. When he tried to pull away, Kyla yanked on his leine to keep him close. Liam groaned as he pulled her even tighter. He used his thumb and forefinger to gently pull her jaw down, and he slid his tongue into her mouth. Her soft moan made his already stiff cock twitch. He wanted nothing more than to plunge into her and discover all the secrets her body held. She was hesitant for a moment about what to do, but she quickly caught on, and their tongues stroked one another. Liam nibbled lightly on her lower lip and was delighted when he felt her lips pull into a smile. He bent lower and moved to kiss her jaw, then down the side of her throat. He made his way back up and felt her hands cup his cheeks. She guided his mouth back to hers and then trailed her hands down his chest until she could wrap her hands around his ribs. The feeling of her running her hands over his back was nearly overwhelming. He walked them backward until her back pressed lightly against the bailey wall.

If I dinna stop this now, I'm going to be tossing her skirts and wrapping her legs around me as I tup her against the wall. This isnae right. She isnae some wench. She's ma wife. Wife? Well, hell, the betrothal papers are signed, we are as good as wed. Which is even more reason I shouldnae be treating her like a whore.

Liam gently pulled back and looked down at her swollen lips. Her passion filled eyes looked up at him with uncertainty. He pressed another quick kiss to her lips, then her nose, and her temple.

"If we dinna stop now, I will be compromising ye against a wall the first day ye're here. I willna dishonor ye, Kyla. Nae ever. I dinna want to stop, but I ken we must."

Kyla's eyes slowly lost the dazed look, and she floated back down to Earth.

"Aye, Liam," she whispered. It was the most she could say.

"Are ye well, lass?"

"Quite," she looked past him and tried to focus on anything that would keep her from pulling him in for another kiss.

"Kyla, I didna mean to accuse ye earlier. That wasna ma intention, but I seem to be making a right mess of every conversation we have. I dinna seem to be able to think straight when I'm near ye, but I wanted ye to ken ye dinna have to hide aught from me. I dinna want ye to fear me or how I might react if ye bring something to ma attention. I dinna think ye are a liar either. Ye may think badly of me, and ye have every right to, but I dinna want ye to believe I think badly of ye."

Liam watched Kyla as she nodded but still seemed far away.

"Kyla—"

"I've never been kissed before."

It was as though she was talking to herself and only realized she spoke aloud once she was done. She looked up at Liam as if she was surprised to find someone listening.

"I probably shouldnae say so, but that makes me incredibly happy to hear."

Kyla's brow furrowed as she looked up at him.

"Did ye think me loose? That I kiss men I've only just met as a habit?" The dusky rose color that filled her cheeks drained to chalk white.

Liam pulled her back against his chest and stroked her hair. Kyla relaxed when she heard the steady beat of his heart. She breathed in his scent and found it calming and enticing all rolled up into one.

"The thought never crossed ma mind. I kenned ye were inexperienced from the way the kiss started, but I was also thrilled to feel ye want ma kiss as much as I want yers. I am simply selfish, and I like kenning I have something nay one else ever has. I want it all for maself, and I am glad to ken I dinna have to share. I could strut around crowing like a rooster because I am the only mon to have kissed ye and the only mon who ever will. I dinna think of maself as a possessive mon, but I find I just might be a wee bit."

She took in everything he told her, and while a warm rush of emotions flowed through her, she felt a chill creep into her heart and mind when she realized she could not say the same about him, there was probably nothing intimate she could claim as her own. She tried to take a step back, and Liam released her immediately. She turned her head to the side because she did not want him to see how much her thoughts bothered her. When his fingers gently tried to turn her head, she shook it.

"I told ye I amnae a liar, and I dinna intend to be deceitful, so I willna start now. I ken it shouldnae bother me, but I find I dinna care for kenning I will never be able to say the same aboot aught we do."

"What do ye mean?"

She looked back at him then as she felt her anger spike again. Was he mocking her or truly that dense?

"I may be a virgin, but I would be a fool to think ye are. This may be all new to me, but I am sure it isnae new to ye. It's all the same to ye, as it has been before when this is a first for me, I—"

Liam pulled her in for another kiss. This one was demanding and possessive. It gave no quarter and demanded none. Liam pressed his tongue against her lips and when she opened them a crack, he pressed forward. His tongue swept the inside of her mouth searching for any part it had not yet found. He gripped her waist and lifted her, so she was eye level. She wrapped her arms around his neck and held on. As his tongue laved hers, she gently sucked on it. Liam's responding growl fueled her to be more brazen, and she sucked harder. He wrapped one arm around her, so he could push his sporran out of the way. He pressed his hips into her, making sure she could not doubt his attraction for her. She moaned as she pressed her hips forward to meet his. She could feel his stiff cock brushing against her lower belly, and it was creating a fire and ache that burned low in her core. Liam's hand spread across one side of her buttocks to squeeze and knead. He groaned as he discovered how lush and soft her curves were. He was beyond pleased to learn one side of her bottom more than filled his large hand. His other hand slid down, so he could firmly hold both sides. This made it easier for Kyla to get the friction she yearned for. Her mind did not understand this craving, but her body did.

 Liam could not believe how close he was to climaxing. He had never spilled his seed without someone touching him. He rocked his hips and ground his cock against her. If he did not stop soon he would spill his seed right there and then. When one of Kyla's hands ran through his hair and held tightly while the other cupped his cheek, he was thoroughly lost. There was something about the mix of tenderness and possessiveness of her hold that made him surrender. He felt his seed spill from him, thankful he had his plaid to hide behind. Kyla's soft moans were not only sounds of pleasure but also ones of frustration. Liam gripped her buttocks tightly and pressed her hard against his still rigid staff. He rocked against her until he felt her go stiff in his arms for a moment and then grow limp. He slowly lowered her to the ground cradling her head in his hand.

 "Mo leannan, I havenae ever done that before."
 "I dinna understand. How could ye nae have? Ye've been

with plenty of other women."

"I wouldnae say plenty, and I meant I have never spilled maself simply from being pressed up against a woman. Neither have I ever felt such overwhelming arousal and uncontrollable desire before either." He leaned back, so he could look down at Kyla and found she was looking up at him. "I canna change ma past because it was before I even kenned ye existed, but I can swear to ye I havenae been with a woman since I found out about our betrothal, and I willna ever stray from ye. The Sinclair men are always faithful to their wives, and I can honestly say I dinna think I could ever find a woman I would desire enough to stray from ye. I wouldnae dishonor either of us in such a way, and I simply canna picture ever wanting anyone else. What we did, what I felt, is unlike aught I have ever felt or done before. I dinna make a habit of seducing women I've only just met, and I dinna make a habit of compromising virgins. Ye throw me off kilter, mo leannan. I think ye have woven a spell around me and bewitched me."

"Liam," her voice was barely above a whisper, "I believe ye about yer honor, and so I believe ye think ye will always be faithful, but what if ye discover I amnae enough? What about when the novelty of bedding a virgin dims? Ye may believe and intend now to never stray, but ye canna predict the future any better than the next mon."

"Oh Kyla, ma sweet, I dinna even ken where to start with that. I dinna want ye to ever, nae for even a moment, think ye arenae enough for me or for anyone. Do ye ken what I have learned about ye in the afternoon we have spent together? And I dinna mean any of the physical intimacies. I have learned ye have a sharp and wicked sense of humor. Ye can take pleasure in nature and appreciate the beauty that surrounds us. Ye are vera observant, and where I seem to utterly lack tact, ye give thought before ye speak. Ye have an ingrained sense of duty and responsibility, and ye hands prove ye arenae afraid of hard work. I love that ye have a temper, and ye arenae afraid to show me. I never want ye to fear me or feel ye must hide aught from me. While I want to ken more about yer life before coming here, I can respect ye maynae be ready to tell me. I dinna think ye are evasive but rather circumspect and cautious.

"I take ma role as ma father's heir and future laird of this clan with utmost seriousness. It may have been a blessing of birth that I am the oldest and will inherit, but it is by choice that I uphold ma clan's values. One of those is faithfulness. It extends beyond ma duties to lead and protect ma clan. It extends to the person I pledge to share ma life with. I wouldnae disgrace maself, ma parents, ma wife, or ma clan by straying. I canna imagine doing something so dishonorable and shameful, and I wouldnae blame the clan for losing trust in me if I did. I wouldnae do that to any woman I marry, and I couldnae do it to ye."

Liam paused to brush hair from Kyla's cheek before tucking it behind her ear.

"I speak the truth when I say I canna imagine ever meeting another woman who could make me feel the way ye have in barely one day. I dinna only mean desire either. Kyla, ye have certainly bewitched me, and I wouldnae have it any differently."

Liam did not intend to say so much; however, he found himself wanting to confess as much to reassure her that not only would he be a devoted husband, but he could already see what a fine woman she was.

"Ye see all of that in me? Already?" She watched as Liam swallowed and nodded his head.

"Do ye ken what I have learned about ye?" Liam shook his head and such a look of dread crossed his face, she could not help but laugh. She drew a fingertip between his brows and down to the bridge of his nose. "Dinna frown, it doesnae make ye any fiercer and will only give ye wrinkles." Her soft peal of laughter had him pinching her waist.

"Dinna make me laugh, or I willna be able to speak."

Liam plastered the most serious expression on his face he could, and that only brought on gales of laughter from Kyla. She clapped both hands over her mouth and peered around his shoulders to be sure they had not drawn any attention to themselves. When she was sure she could speak without being overcome, she moved her hands away.

"I have learned nae only can ye make jests at yer own expense, but ye also arenae afraid to be silly. Ye may take yer duties and responsibilities seriously, but ye dinna always take yerself too seriously. I ken ye can feel contrite and guilty when ye err, and ye arenae too prideful to admit to yer faults and ask forgiveness. I ken ye are protective and will use yer size to shield me, but I dinna think ye would ever use yer size against me. I dinna fear ye at all. Just the opposite, despite being an arse when ye dinna ken I could hear ye, ye have already proven ye are trustworthy. We are already betrothed, and many men would consider that as good as married which would entitle them to bed me. Ye have stopped us before we could go too far, nae once but twice. Ye may desire me, and I might add I clearly desire ye even if I dinna fully understand it, but ye are still trying to protect me. Ye are just possessive enough to make me feel wanted, but ye dinna strike me as the type to be so possessive as to be controlling. Instead, I think ye respect me. I think ye respect me as ye would any woman ye were to marry, but I think ye also respect ma opinion and ma own honor. Ye may be the brawest mon I have ever met, nae ever even seen, but ye are also proving to be one of the best."

Liam leaned forward and rested his forehead against hers and the tips of their noses together. He breathed in the lemongrass fragrance and knew that scent would forever onward only be associated with the woman he was rapidly falling for.

"Brawest, am I?" he said with a chuckle, "Do ye ken I've already realized ye are the bonniest woman I have ever laid eyes on? I kenned it the moment I saw ye, but now that I actually ken ye, I see yer outer beauty is a mere hint of yer inner beauty."

Kyla pulled back and stepped away.

"Liam, ye dinna have to exaggerate. I already believe ye. Dinna ruin this by gilding the lily and giving false compliments."

"What false compliments? I havenae said aught that isnae true. What could I have made up?"

"I am nay great beauty. I never have been, nor do I think I will be any time soon. Ye dinna have to make things up to win me over. Quite the opposite." She wrapped her arms around her middle. Liam could not imagine a more protective stance that did not involve a weapon.

"Kyla, now it is ma turn to nae understand. How can ye think ye arenae beautiful? Have ye never seen yer own reflection?"

"Of course, I have seen ma own reflection, and I ken I am too short, too broad about the hips, ma nose is too flat, and ma breasts are obscene for a noblewoman. I ken ma hair looks like a crow's wing and that it is a blessing I am strong enough to do ma fair share of work, or I wouldnae earn a place at the table."

Liam stood with his mouth agape and then shut and opened it several more times before he could manage to string a coherent thought together enough to say anything. He looked at Kyla utterly dumbfounded. He finally shook his head to clear his mind before wrapping his very large hand around her very tiny wrist and dragged her out into the bailey. Unlike Kyla, whose head was on a swivel to see who might have noticed they left a secluded spot together, Liam was singularly focused on his destination. He towed Kyla along until he reached the smithy. He pounded on the doorframe, but the noise of the fires and bellows was too loud. He practically dragged Kyla into the large workroom. He scanned the various pieces of metal lying around until he found a large piece of shiny, unshaped steel. He nearly yanked her arm out as he positioned her in front of him. He held the metal up in front of them.

"Look. Take a good long look into this and tell me how ye can possibly think ye arenae the most beautiful woman in the Highlands, nay, all of Scotland, if nae the entire Christian world." He shook his head. "Dinna be modest either. Tell me how ye canna see what is vera obvious to me."

Kyla peered into the polished metal and saw what she always saw. She did not understand what Liam was talking about. She still saw all the same flaws that had been pointed out to her time and again, year after year. She shook her head and pushed his hands away. She ducked under his arm and ran out of the smithy. She ran across the bailey and almost made it to the steps before Liam caught up to her.

"Kyla, wait. Christ's bones, I should add fleet-footed to yer already long list of attributes. Why did ye run? I used to think I was a fairly bright and astute mon, but I have in the past day come to realize I'm dafter than a hound chasing its own tail."

Eyes watering, Kyla could only shake her head. She walked up the steps to the keep's doors and paused before entering. Liam watched as she straightened her spine and swept her sleeve across her eyes. She lifted her chin and reached for the door.

Liam ran a hand through his hair, making it stand on end, before putting his hands on his hips. He did not know if he should chase her again or give her some space. The highs and lows of the afternoon suddenly left him feeling exhausted. He knew Kyla had not done anything wrong but only ever reacted to his words and actions. He simply did not understand many of these reactions, but he did know there were things from her past that clearly left deep, if not invisible wounds. Before her, there had never been a woman he cared enough about or been interested enough to want to find the cause nor want to be the balm.

He stared up at the doors she passed through wondering what he should do next.

Bluidy hell. I've mucked it up. Again. The lass deserves a reprieve from me, and I deserve a dunk in the bluidy cold loch.

CHAPTER THREE

Kyla entered the Great Hall and prayed she could find someone, anyone, who could point her in the direction of her chamber. She did not want to talk to anyone except for the least amount of words needed to learn where her destination was.

The first person she came across was Lady Arabella. Kyla wanted to groan. Arabella was the last person she wanted to talk to, but the only person she could not avoid. Arabella took one look at Kyla and drew her aside.

"What has ma son said now? Ye ken ma husband is a brilliant mon. He's a strong leader and provider for his family and clan, he's a master tactician, the bravest warrior I have ever met, and the brawest mon I have ever seen, but he is also utterly unaware of how to converse with women. Liam is his father's son. I can only guess what he may have said or done to upset ye again, but I guarantee it wasnae meant to be malicious. The path to hell is paved with good intentions, and Liam is chalked full of them."

Arabella watched Kyla closely and saw the slight tremble of her hands despite the head held high and the ramrod straight back.

"I doubt ye have heard the story of how Donnell and I

came to be married. We met at a clan gathering the summer I was ten summers, and he was thirteen summers. I still dinna ken exactly how a boy on the cusp of being a mon took such an interest in a child, but I thank God daily that he did. The clan gathering was unusually long and ran for a fortnight. During that time, Donnell and I were inseparable except for when duty absolutely dictated we be with our families. Right before the end of the gathering, Donnell convinced his sisters to suggest to their mother I come to foster here. Lady Sinclair agreed, and she was able to convince ma father and mother.

"I arrived within a sennight, and we picked up where we left off, but over the course of the next five summers, Donnell grew more distant as his training increased. It was natural he would want to spend more time with the other young guardsmen, but it hurt to feel ignored. What's worse was I started hearing the serving girls talk about him and how vera handsome he was. It was always followed by unchaste suggestions as to what they would like to do. As if hearing aboot that at every turn in this keep wasna bad enough, the rumors of him at the village tavern started to trickle back. Apparently, as a one, the young guardsmen quite enjoyed going into the village to drink and carouse.

"One afternoon, I had a massive stack of recently darned and mended leines for the single guardsmen, and I was sent to deliver them. As I approached, the door to the barracks was open, and I could hear several young men talking. They were teasing someone, but I didna realize who until I was close enough to see inside the room. I could see Donnell, and I was curious, so I stood around the corner from the door. He was the one they were teasing, and it was about why he did *nae* take up with any of the women who practically threw themselves at him. I will never forget his answer, 'why would I bother with any of them when I already ken who I'm going to marry.' I stood there as ma heart broke into a thousand pieces. I was sure they must have heard them shatter to the ground, but instead, I must have moved slightly. One of the guardsmen thought I just arrived and called me in. I went in and held up the stack of leines because I couldnae squeeze out a single word. Thomas, one of the oldest in the group, cornered me against the door frame and asked why I didna come around more often and told me I would always be welcome. He reached out to touch ma hair as he asked me to go for a walk with him that evening. His hand brushed the side of ma breast, and the next thing I kenned, Donnell had him pinned against the door with a dirk to his throat. He was beyond livid. I have never, even to this day, seen him so angry about aught. He told Thomas, 'dinna ever speak that way again to the woman I'll wed. I will gut ye and nae think twice.' When he let Thomas go, he grabbed ma wrist and practically dragged me into an alley a few buildings down," Arabella gave Kyla a pointed look and raised an eyebrow.

At the mention of the alley, Kyla suddenly remembered she dropped her bouquet while they were there. She desperately wanted to go back and look for it, hoping it was uncrushed, but she did her best to keep listening to Arabella's story.

"Donnell kissed me for the first time right then and there. I burst into tears when he apologized for the way Thomas spoke to me and that he would never let it happen again. Donnell tried to reassure me nay other mon would ever be so dishonorable to me, and I could have punched him at that moment. When I didna stop crying, he finally asked me what was wrong. I still remember what I said, too. 'It's ye. If ye hadnae been ignoring me for the past few summers, and if ye hadnae been off carousing and carrying on with other women, or at least letting the entire clan think ye were, nay mon would have spoken that way to me, and I wouldnae be crying.' Donnell could have been blown over by a feather. He told me aboot how he was waiting until I was older, and he thought he would have to woo me. He had absolutely nay idea I was as in love with him as he was with me. He had nay idea I heard any of the talk or rumors, and he had nay idea how his distance hurt me. He thought I was simply busy with other tasks in and around the keep, and they would be enough to keep me occupied until I was old enough to be courted.

"Anyway, Kyla, the point of ma story is both ma husband and son are more than any woman could ever ask for in the way of provider and protector, but they are as dense as fog over a bog when it comes to understanding how women think and feel. Donnell still makes a mess of things quite regularly, and we've been wed for twenty-five summers. Give Liam a chance. He didna make a vera good first impression, but he is a good mon. He is going to trip up from time to time and come across as insensitive, but that isnae what he really is. It usually happens when he is out of his depth."

Arabella leaned forward to hug Kyla, and she welcomed it. She lost her mother when she was young, and it eased a great burden to suddenly have a woman who might be able to fill that hollow spot in her life.

"Are ye wanting to go to yer chamber?"

"Nay, or at least nae yet. I just remembered I dropped something."

Kyla did not wait for Arabella's answer but spun on her heel and dashed out of the keep. She walked as quickly as she could short of running. When she reached the shadows of the buildings, she did run. She breathed a sigh of relief when she spotted the flowers on the ground, and they were still in good condition. She picked them up and blew off the dust the petals captured. She sniffed the bouquet as she moved back towards the sunlight. She was so distracted she did not think to look before she emerged from between the buildings. It was not until she heard voices that she looked over to the group of women congregated around the well. They were all looking at her, and Kyla knew in that instant, they were speculating about who she met in the alley. Kyla also knew by the evening meal there would be rumors abounding about how the laird's son's betrothed was caught leaving a tryst.

She had to find Liam. She looked around the bailey but

could not see him. He had not passed her in the Great Hall, and she did not think he went into the kitchens. She was starting to panic when the smithy stepped out and came to stand beside her.

"He went out the postern gate to the loch. Lass, I dinna ken what he said to ye before ye came in, and I couldnae hear all of what he said to ye inside, but it doesnae take a scholar to see the mon is vera smitten with ye. I dinna think he meant to hurt ye. I think he meant exactly the opposite."

Kyla looked at the man and saw a kindly face that was weathered and tan. He nodded his head in the direction of the back gate, and she smiled. Once again, she lifted her chin and squared her back before walking past the gaggle of women who made no effort to hide they were talking about her. She slipped out of the gate and looked around. When she spotted a path that she was sure would take her to the loch, she followed it.

She reached the bottom of the hill in front of the loch when she heard splashing. She turned to look and gasped.

Liam was walking out of the water without a stitch of clothing on. She had never seen a man fully undressed before, and it was the most magnificent sight she ever beheld. He was pushing back his hair when he spotted her standing there staring. She knew she should look away, but he was like a magnet to her eyes. She watched as his muscles bunched and shifted as he approached. She marveled at how from waist up his skin was sun-kissed, and even his calves and feet were too, but from waist to knee he was much paler. Once she noticed that, she could not help noticing what hung between his legs and gasped again. First, she saw the thatch of dark hair and then the very protrusion she felt earlier that day. Except earlier, there was a plaid to separate them, and now there was absolutely nothing.

Liam heard a noise as he made his way to shore, but when he looked up, Kyla was the last thing he expected to see. The more he hurried to reach his plaid, the wider her eyes became.

He could see her eyes moving over him, and he almost chuckled when she gasped again as her eyes lowered to his waist. Her mouth formed a perfect oh, and he could have jumped back into the loch. The sight was enough to immediately make him picture what she would look like and what it would feel like to have her lips encircling his cock as the smooth tongue he explored earlier caressed him. He could not help his body's reaction as his imagination ran away. He felt himself growing, so he ran the last few steps to grab his plaid, which he quickly slung around his waist before pulling on his leine.

Liam looked around to make sure no one could see them. He knew he already compromised her, but he did not want any of the clan to think so. He took her hand and guided them behind a group of rocks big enough to shield them from the view of the keep or anyone walking nearby.

"Lass, what are ye doing out here?"

Kyla could only stare at his chest. She felt her cheeks flame, her mouth went dry, and she was sure she drooled at least once. She tried to discreetly check the corner of her mouth by pretending she was moving a strand of hair. She almost sighed when she realized she had not actually drooled, though she would not have been surprised if she had.

"Kyla?"

"Aye?"

"What are ye doing out here, lass?"

"Oh well, I needed to find ye."

"I would certainly say ye have. Why did ye need to find me?" Liam could not keep from chuckling at her distracted answers. "Kyla, ye were looking for me?"

"I needed to speak to ye." She shook her head and tried to focus on what he was saying and not what he looked like. She had to fist the hand not holding the flowers to keep from reaching out and touching him. "After I went inside, I ran into yer mother, and she told me the story of how she met yer father, and it made me remember I dropped ma flowers, and it was so vera important to me to get them back, so I went to the alley to get them, and when I came out of the shadows, I didna look around, and some women saw me, and now I am sure they will be telling all and sundry I was trysting with someone."

She heaved a breath when she finished. She spoke so fast Liam was not entirely sure he caught everything.

"Slow down, Kyla. Ye went into the keep but left again because ye remembered aboot the flowers," he gestured to the bouquet in her hand, "and after ye picked them up, some women saw ye. Why do ye think they will be talking about ye?"

"Liam, yer mother told me ye could be thick when it comes to women, and I thought as much, but I didna ken how right she was. Liam, what were we doing when we were in that alley? That's exactly what those women thought I was doing too, but when ye didna step out with me, and I did with a bouquet in ma hands, well, I can only imagine what nasty things they are saying. They're going to say I was meeting some mon, and the laird's son is marrying an unchaste woman. That's why I needed to find ye, to tell ye before ye heard the wrong version of the story from someone else. I swear to ye there wasna anyone else there. I only picked up the flowers and left. I promise."

"Kyla, I ken. Or at least, I ken ye wouldnae be meeting anyone else there. I wouldnae believe those rumors anyway. I already kenned ye forgot the flowers, so that's why I was coming out of the loch. I was going to fetch them for ye."

"That might be so, but that willna stop the nashgab once it gets started. Women are cruel when it comes to gossip, and I am new here. I wouldnae be surprised either if there arenae a slew of women who are nae too pleased ye are supposed to be marrying me and nae them."

"What do ye mean supposed to be? Of course, I'm marrying ye."

"Ye are the future laird. Ye canna marry someone whose

morals are in question. Say we did wed, and I got with child quickly, what then? People would question whether the bairn was yers. And God forbid we have a son first. People who question his right to inherit. They might claim he's a bastard once ye're gone. Oh, Liam. I wasna thinking when I stepped out. I was—I was thinking aboot us, and I was distracted."

Liam grinned before asking, "And what were ye thinking aboot that had ye so distracted."

Kyla looked up at him and wanted to wipe the smug look from his face, but instead, she sighed, and her shoulders drooped.

"I was thinking aboot what yer mother told me, and that mayhap I overreacted at the smithy's. Then, once I had the flowers again, I couldnae stop thinking aboot the way ye made me feel when ye touched me. And when I touched ye too."

Liam drew her into his arms and set the bouquet on the rocks next to them.

"Kyla, I already told ye today I ken ye're nae a liar. I dinna think ye are now, and I dinna think ye're loose. I wouldnae have believed it anyway, if nae for the simple fact I watched ye go into the keep, I didna see ye leave immediately, and I was barely in the water for five minutes. There isnae any way ye had time to tryst with anyone. I am going to marry ye, nae because it was arranged, but because I vera much want to. Much has happened in the space of a day, but I also feel like I have gotten to ken much aboot ye in these mere few hours. I dinna understand all I have learned, but I have liked all of it. I like ye, lass. Let anyone say aught about ye, and they will quickly learn I protect what's mine."

Liam's mouth sank to hers with a kiss that began softly, but the moment she opened for him, became fierce, possessive, and passionate. They were laying claim to one another. Liam grasped her backside and lifted her off the ground. She wrapped her legs around his waist, and he turned to rest her on a rock. He settled into the vee of her legs and pressed his stiff cock against her. He rubbed against her creating the friction he already knew she enjoyed. He kissed her jaw and throat, working his way down to the flesh that swelled over the top of her neckline. Her hands ran over his hair, his shoulders, and as far down his back as she could reach. She crossed her ankles and arched her back. She moaned softly as she felt Liam's tongue dip below the top of her kirtle, and he continued to press his hips forward. She did not understand why she ached so badly low in her belly, but the pressure he gave helped quell her need, if only slightly.

He could not get enough of her. He already spent himself once without her touching his cock, and he was about to do it again even though he took himself in hand after diving into the loch. He could feel the need for release growing quickly. He thrust harder and faster.

"Kyla, I want to be inside ye so badly. I want to feel ye around me, and I want to make ye find yer release as I did before. Lass, do ye trust me? I willna take yer maidenhead, but I will bring ye pleasure. Will ye let me?"

Kyla could only nod her head as the sensations coursing through her were nearly too much. Liam slid his hand up the inside of her thigh and nearly spent himself when his fingers found the moisture his staff longed to feel. He pressed one finger inside her to test that she was ready and that he would not frighten her. Her hips lifted off the rock, and she pressed down on his hand. He slid a second finger in and slowly began to stroke her sensitive nub with his thumb. Her head shot up as she looked at him.

"Liam?" She panted.

"Aye, mo leannan. Sshh, dinna fash. Let go and let yerself feel." He pressed his mouth gently against hers as he pressed harder on her sensitive skin. He was rewarded with a moan, and she intensified the kiss by biting his lower lip. She lowered her head back to the rock and brought him with her as she fisted his leine.

Kyla could feel a wave growing inside as it had earlier against the wall.

"More. I dinna ken what, but oh God, more, Liam."

In response to her plea, he added a third finger, excited by the feeling of how tight her channel was. He continued to rock his hips against her and the back of his hand. He knew he was going to climax without her even touching him. Again. That had never happened to him before let alone twice in one afternoon. His desire for this woman grew exponentially as his interest and tenderness grew within his chest.

He stroked faster as he leaned away. He knew she was close, and the shadows of the building earlier cheated him of the chance to watch her face as she found her own release. He was not disappointed as he watched the flush rise from her chest, her breathing became shorter and faster, and her eyes closed with a look of pure bliss on her face. He could no longer hold back. He felt the streams shoot from him as his cock twitched over and over. It was the greatest climax he ever experienced, and he was not even inside her. He could not fathom what it would be like once they were wed and could fully explore and enjoy.

Bracing himself on his forearms, he leaned over her when she pulled him closer. She wrapped herself around him. He brushed her hair back from her face where a short tendril stuck to her damp skin, and he kissed the sensitive skin at the base of her neck. He breathed in lemongrass.

After what was probably several minutes but felt like only seconds to Liam, he heard her timid voice. It was a tone he never heard before.

"Liam?"

"Mo leannan?"

"I dinna understand what happened to me. It happened earlier, but I dinna ken why I felt such a wave of pleasure. I havenae ever felt aught like it. "

"Sweetheart, how old were ye when yer mother died?"

"I was twelve summers."

"Ye were still too young for yer mother to have explained

what happens between a mon and a woman when their bodies come together."

Kyla ducked her head, embarrassed to be talking about what she clearly should have known.

"Kyla, look at me. There isnae aught to be ashamed of. We will be married soon and share a bed every night. There is much we will learn about one another's bodies."

Kyla bit her lower lip and did not stop herself. Liam gently pulled it loose.

"Ye're nervous, and that's fine, but dinna hide from me," Liam said softly.

"I was twelve summers when ma courses started. All ma mother said was I could now breed, and I mustnae disgrace maself or ma clan by having a bastard. I didna understand until a few years later. Liam, I've lived in a large castle ma entire life. I couldnae escape seeing people or animals couple. I understand what happens. I just dinna understand what I felt."

"Ye didna have any other women ye could have talked to before being sent off to wed? Nay one to prepare ye?"

"Molly, our housekeeper, said I am to accept ma husband's attention whenever he wants, and I should expect and accept his attention would be spent on others more often than on me. She said I was to only lie there until I'd birthed an heir and a spare. Then ma husband would leave me alone. She said only whores enjoyed coupling, and since I'm the laird's daughter, I shouldnae ever be a whore. But Liam, I did enjoy it. I dinna want ye to think me wanton or loose."

Liam scooped her off the rock and held her in his arms as he lowered them to the ground. He arranged her in his lap before he thought about what he should say next.

"Naught of that is true or right. Enjoying being with a mon doesnae make ye a whore. It means ye are the way God made ye to be. If it wasna what He intended, then yer body wouldnae feel that pleasure. That feeling was yer climax, yer release. It's natural, and it means yer body was satisfied. I wanted ye to feel that. I wanted ye to be pleasured, and I wanted to ken I was the one, the only one, to give ye that. Kyla, touching ye and kissing ye alone was enough for me to spend ma seed both times we've been together and shared intimacies. Ye've already given me more pleasure than I've ever felt before, and ye havenae even touched me yet. What we share together is for us and is ours alone. I dinna ever want ye to feel like ye're obligated to couple with me. I dinna want it to be a duty for ye. I willna ask ye to do aught ye dinna want or enjoy. I would only ask that ye tell me what ye do enjoy. I will always strive to bring ye as much pleasure as ye do for me."

Kyla rested her head against his shoulder and felt herself relax.

"Liam, how can it be that I feel like I've kenned ye a lifetime, but it hasnae even been a day? Is it simply lust because ye are the brawest, most handsome mon I have ever seen? Isnae lust a sin?"

"It can be when ye covet someone ye arenae supposed to desire. It is if it drives ye hurt to someone. But it isnae a sin between husband and wife. I canna explain it either. I admit at first, I was struck by yer beauty. Ye took ma breath away, but I feel the same as ye. It's as though I've spent ma entire life waiting for ye, but at the same time, I feel like there's never been a time before ye."

Kyla sighed and ran her fingers over the exposed skin where the laces to his leine were undone. Liam twirled a lock of her hair around his finger.

"Lass, when do ye wish to marry? I would do it today if ye wanted, but I will willingly wait until ye feel ready."

"I dinna ken. The bands have been read, so it could be today, but I dinna think that's wise. So much has happened today, it's a bit overwhelming. I dinna want either of us to wake up in the morn and regret being rash. I want to get to ken ye better to be a good wife to ye. I dinna even ken yer favorite color or yer favorite food. Or if there is a food ye canna stand.

"Green, carrots, liver. And ye are wise beyond yer years. We will wait until ye say ye're ready. Only then will we wed. I willna let anyone pressure ye into marrying me if ye dinna feel it's right."

Kyla reached out and cupped his chin. She kissed him with such tenderness that he wanted to place her inside a bubble where he could always protect her. His chest ached with a feeling that was completely new to him.

CHAPTER FOUR

"Will ye look at the tits on that one?"

Liam was not interested in anything his cousin, Randall, had to say. His father's sister, husband, and children arrived while he was at the loch. Supposedly, they came to be sure they did not miss the wedding. Liam suspected it was to live off his mother and father's hospitality. His uncle, Shamus MacDougall, was notoriously tight-fisted with money, and his Aunt Ellen was a spendthrift. Any chance to feed his family for free, even as a laird, appealed to him. Randall was their only son and spoiled his entire life. He was a lecher who sired bastards across half of the Highlands. Liam only tolerated him for the sake of his father and his aunt, who he was rather fond of.

"And look at those hips and arse. Plenty to hold onto while I'm pumping her from behind. I've never seen a wench with such black hair."

Liam saw red. There was only one woman who would be in the keep with dark black hair. His vision tunneled and everything else faded to black. He kicked back the bench he was sitting on and came over the table. He grabbed his cousin by the throat and lifted him off his feet. He pushed him the few steps to the beam behind Randall's back. He thrust him so hard against the wood Randall's head made a sick thud. He shifted his arm to pin him by the throat. His other arm jabbed forward into the other man's belly. He pulled back and rammed his fist into Randall's nose creating a satisfying crack as it broke. The third punch broke Randall's jaw, and the fourth blackened his eye.

"Dinna ever, ever speak aboot ma bride like that again. If I find ye've uttered another filthy word aboot her, I will gut ye like a stuffed pig. Kin or nae. Do ye understand me?"

Randall let out a choking sound and could barely nod his head. Liam lowered him and tossed him aside. He was still filled with battle lust. The only reason not to kill Randall on the spot, despite years of loathing and the crass comments he heard moments ago, was because they were family. The last thing his clan needed was a feud with his family by marriage.

He felt a small warm hand on the bare skin of his forearm. He looked down to see Kyla staring up at him. Her face was pale, and her teeth were pressed so deeply into her lower lip they would surely leave marks.

The fight went out of Liam the moment he recognized fear in her eyes. She slid her hand down to take his and gently pulled him away. She led him out of the Great Hall to stand outside. There was a crispness in the air that helped calm him.

Kyla looked up at him before she wrapped her arms around his middle. She pressed a kiss to his chest and held him. Slowly, his arms came around her as he returned the embrace.

"I dinna want ye to fear me, Kyla. I dinna usually behave like that."

"Mo ghaisgeach, ma warrior, I amnae fearful of ye so much as the consequences of yer anger. I ken ye were defending ma honor, but I dinna want to be the cause of a clan war between family. What did he say?"

"It doesnae bear repeating. Suffice it to say, it was lewd."

"Do ye remember what I told ye when yer mother explained how she and yer father came to be wed? Apparently, something similar happened, and if I remember correctly, ye said almost the same thing as yer father. Ye just did a bit more damage."

Kyla could not help but smile a bit. She knew she should not but seeing the man who had been so caring to her earlier that day, rage like an angry bear made her smile.

"It isnae funny. Ye're right aboot the clan war, but that would have been ma fault nae yers."

"That wasna what I was smiling aboot. I was thinking ye were as sweet as a lamb earlier, and now ye are like a bear that's been stung for sticking his paw in the hive. Mayhap ye are ferocious after all. Nae one has ever stood up for me before," she trailed off in a whisper. "Nae one's ever needed to."

Liam heard the hurt in her voice and remembered back to the disaster that was their trip to the blacksmith. He simply held her as he tried to think of a tactful way to ask her about her family. He was already piecing together quite a bit. Her rough and calloused hands. Her reference to being teased. Her disbelief that she was beautiful. Her surprise that he defended her.

"What was life like before ye came here?"

He felt her go rigid and then it was as though she simply deflated.

"When ma mother died, ma father felt I wasna any use to him until I could marry and bring a bride price and alliance to him. I was sent first to work in the kitchens, then with the laundresses, and finally as a servant within the keep. He claimed it was the best he could do to ensure I was ready to be chatelaine, but I ken that wasna true."

"But what of yer brothers? There's three, arenae there? I told ye I've met them."

"Ma father led by example, so ma brothers were nae much better. Ma middle brother, Hamish, wasna as bad as the others. When we were much younger, he would still talk to me when he came in from the lists. He was never cruel or even unkind, but he became distant when the others gave him a hard time for coddling his wee sister."

"Still talked to ye. Are ye saying yer kin doesnae even talk to ye? Ye said in the Great Hall they teased ye. Did ye mean they taunted ye or belittled ye?

"It hasnae been all bad. I was able to spend some time with the MacLeods when we hosted a Highland gathering. I became vera good friends with the laird's daughter, Rose. We sought each other out any time our clans were together. "

"Lass, how often could that be? Yer own kin didna talk to ye, ye were treated as a servant if nae worse, and ye had one friend ye might have seen once a year. Kyla, that isnae how it's supposed to be."

Liam's heart broke for what she suffered and may not have even known was mistreatment.

"I have one more question, and then I'll leave off. Why do ye think ye arenae beautiful?"

Kyla buried her face in Liam's chest. She knew she held no control over her looks, but it felt like her greatest failure.

"Liam, ye dinna need to flatter me or make things up to make me feel better. I ken what I ken. I told ye before, I am too short, I am too broad across the beam, ma hair looks like a crow's wing and is both flat and dull, and ma breasts are indecent for a noblewoman. Ma nose is too short, and I have teeth like a beaver and a face like a horse. I ken I have hands like a washerwoman, and ma feet are too big for ma height. Besides men dinna like women who have overly large muscles. Ma arms and legs are too wide from the work I have done."

Kyla could not bring herself to look at him, but Liam grasped her shoulder and set her back.

"Who the bluidy hell has been telling ye such a pile of shite?" He was practically yelling by the time he was finished.

Kyla shrugged as best she could with his grip on her shoulders. He eased his hold but did not let go.

"Who hasnae? Ma father, ma brothers and their wives, the

women who work in the keep, and Molly before I left, when she told me how to behave as yer wife."

"Och, she proved to be a right font of information, that one. I dinna ken why anyone would lie to ye in such a horrible way, especially yer own family, but Christ on the cross, they couldnae have been more wrong. Kyla, ye may nae be what other's think of as the perfect looking noblewoman, but ye are exactly what every mon wants. Why do ye think I was enraged by what Randall said? He noticed exactly what I noticed, and I am sure what every other mon with a beating heart has noticed. Ye are buxom with ample curves, and dammit, I canna stop thinking aboot them and what I want to do with ye, to ye. Randall's first mistake was thinking the same thing, and his second mistake was saying them out loud. Ye are what men fantasize aboot, but they often must settle for much less. I am fortunate enough to be the one wedding ye, and so I am the one who benefits most from yer beauty. But lass, even if ye were nae so beautiful on the outside, ye have more beauty on the inside than any other woman I ken. I understand that doesnae mean much when ye think ye arenae as good as other women, but--" He ran his hand through his hair. "I'm rambling now. I dinna ken what else to say besides I wish I could wring yer brothers' and father's necks. Bluidy eejits."

Kyla held her arms out to him again, and he pulled her in. She wrapped her arms around him tightly and would not have let go if Laird and Lady Sinclair did not step outside. They moved apart and released one another.

"There ye are," Donnell said. "That was quite the hurly-burly ye caused in there."

"I caused?" The vein in Liam's neck stuck out.

Kyla put a restraining hand on his chest and shook her head. Liam took a deep breath before wrapping his arm around her waist and pulling her to his side.

"Randall's comments about Kyla were beyond inappropriate. I willna ever back down where ma wife is concerned."

"But, son," his mother interjected, "she isnae yer wife yet, is she?"

He glowered at his mother.

"Liam," Kyla hissed.

He simply pulled her more tightly against him.

"She will be soon enough. She is ma betrothed, and as far as any other mon, or any other person, is concerned, she is as good as married to me already."

Donnell wrapped his arm around his own wife, and whispered none too quietly, "Sounds awfully familiar."

Arabella stretched to her tiptoes, and her husband leaned sideways to her. She pecked him on the cheek.

"The apple dinna fall far, does it, ma love?"

As they turned to go walk back through the doors, Donnell called back over his shoulder, "Dinna dilly dally much longer, or it'll be ye I'm rescuing her from."

With that, they disappeared back into the keep.

Neither Kyla nor Liam seemed to notice her hand still lay on his chest until she tried to pull it away. He covered it with his.

"I will always defend ye. It doesnae matter against whom. Always." He kissed her temple before escorting her back into the keep.

That night, Kyla climbed into the biggest and softest bed she had ever felt. She lay there looking up at the ceiling as she said her nightly prayers. She was simply too exhausted to kneel. When she finished, she thought back over the course of the day.

How did I go from thinking he was boorish and arrogant to thinking I may be falling in love with him? All in the space of one day. How can that even be? I havenae met anyone else like him. I ken I havenae met many men, to begin with, but those I ken from ma own clan are naught like him. Naught are like his father either. I canna reconcile how he can be so gentle with me one moment and ready to kill a mon the next. I suppose that is the way of warriors and what makes them warriors. But even when he is upset, he doesnae intimidate me. Ma brothers and father used to rail against me all the time, and I feared them. Perhaps it's because it hasnae been directed at me. Yet. Mayhap that is when I will see what he is really like. I would marry him tomorrow, but I dinna think that's wise. I think I need to be sure I understand him and what he expects. He may claim he will protect me, but isnae that what ma father and brothers were supposed to do too? I willna purposely test him, that doesnae sit right with me, but I will observe a wee longer.

Kyla drifted off to sleep thinking about all she saw and learned about Liam and the Sinclair clan. There was only one thing that niggled at the back of her mind, but she assured herself Liam had already taken care of it.

Surely, Randall willna be a problem again.

Liam lay in bed looking at the ceiling, knowing Kyla occupied the chamber directly above his. The keep was well made, and noise did not travel well through the walls or the floor, but he was sure he could hear her moving about and then the bed creak when she laid down. He turned on his side and stretched out his hand to the empty side of his bed. He had never brought a woman to his chamber before. He would not be so disrespectful to his mother, and his father taught him that the bed in his chamber was a sacred space reserved only for his wife. Now that he knew who that would be, he could not help but picture her there.

I canna believe I am truly looking forward to seeing the same face every eve and every morn. I havenae ever wanted to share this space with anyone before, so it was never a hardship to seek ma pleasure elsewhere. But now, I find maself vera impatient for her to move in here.

He climbed out of bed and found his sporran. He lifted a long, thick stalk of lemongrass from it. He had surreptitiously pushed one into his sporran as he cut flowers for Kyla earlier. He got back into bed and laid the plant on the pillow next to his.

Lord God, thank ye for the many blessings ye have bestowed upon me. I have loving parents and a strong clan I pray I will one day lead as well as ma father and his father before him have done. But the greatest blessing ye have given me so far is Kyla. Lord, make me worthy of being her husband. Give me the strength to help her realize her own worth and guide me to nae muck it up any more. She is ma greatest treasure.

CHAPTER FIVE

The next two weeks passed in a blur for both Kyla and Liam. The mornings were spent in the lists for Liam. He trained harder than he ever had before. His impending role as a husband made him realize other roles such as father and laird were much closer than he ever before considered. He felt there was more at stake now, and he pushed himself to be faster, stronger, better not for his own gain but for the men he already led into battle and the ones he was sure to lead again. In the back of his mind was also an overwhelming need for Kyla to be proud of him. The idea of disappointing her any more than he did the day they met was gut-wrenching.

While Liam worked in the lists, Kyla spent her mornings with Arabella. Liam's mother was warm and loving in a way Kyla had not even experienced with her own mother. Arabella asked for Kyla's opinion often, considered it carefully, and more often than not agreed with it. They spent most of the first week touring the keep and introducing Kyla to the various members of the clan and their duties within the bailey walls. Kyla felt comfortable mentioning to Arabella what she saw with the laundresses. It turned out the head laundress was bedridden for several weeks with gout, and it was her much less experienced daughter, Bethea, who took over. She was a shrew who no one liked, and everyone took pity on her husband, Andrew, who ran the armory. None of the other women mustered the fortitude to go up against her and correct her about the soap. While the information may have come from Kyla, Arabella quietly pointed out this was not the battle to win first. Making an enemy of Bethea would serve none of them, so it was Arabella who pointed out the soap recipe was not quite right.

The second week found them with a little more time to sit together and talk while they sewed. Arabella was in the middle of a tapestry, and she was impressed with both Kyla's weaving and embroidery skills. They often worked in companionable silence, but just as often, they talked about members of the clan who lived in the village and their various needs. They discussed what types of root vegetables would be best this season to store, how much grain would be needed to make it through the winter, and how many cows would need to be slaughtered to have a ready stock of dried beef anytime men rode out. Arabella was repeatedly impressed that Kyla's knowledge went far beyond most young women's, even those trained to be chatelaine of such a large castle. Arabella quickly picked up that this knowledge could only have been gathered through firsthand experience.

When she mentioned as much to her husband, he kissed her on the forehead and asked why she thought he inquired about a possible marriage to the lass. He admitted he heard rumors about Kyla being mistreated by her family, but he also heard she was far superior to any other woman her age in running a household the same size as the Sinclairs'.

A little before the nooning, Liam would return from the lists, by way of a wash at the loch, and spend the rest of the afternoon and early evening with Kyla. They went for walks through the village where many of the crofters greeted her by name and even some with hugs. Liam was impressed she made such a strong impression on so many that quickly. Highlanders were not known for being particularly welcoming to newcomers and were often suspicious of outsiders; however, Kyla clearly won them all over. She quietly whispered repairs and improvements she noticed, and Liam was often surprised and even embarrassed that he did not notice these things first. When he asked how she knew so much, she simply shrugged and said it was something she was used to doing. He held his tongue, but he desperately wanted to point out these were things her father and brothers should have taken responsibility for.

They also spent many afternoons out riding. Liam discovered she was an excellent rider, and a daredevil too.

"This is *Seggr*, he has carried me through many a battle and lives up to his name. He is ma hero." Liam rubbed the nose of a giant chestnut stallion. He was easily the biggest horse in both height and girth Kyla had ever seen. She looked from owner to horse and back again and could not help but think how fitting it was that a man as large as Liam would have such a massive animal. Liam moved into the stall and began to saddle his horse. Kyla looked around and spotted her own horse a few stalls down. As she turned, she saw a barrel of carrots nearby. She pulled two out and came back in front of *Seggr*.

"Ye are a handsome mon. I shall be vera lucky to ride with ye today. Be sure to behave."

"Lass, when have I ever beha—" Liam stopped in horror as he watched his half-ton horse nuzzle her hand and eat the carrot with more care than since he was a colt. "How'd ye do that? He doesnae like anyone but me. Even then, he doesnae always like me."

"Apparently, I have a way with men." She slipped over to her own horse's stall before Liam could reach her.

Liam watched as she entered the stall of a large horse he had seen a few times recently and assumed was a new purchase by his father. Kyla made short work of saddling the horse herself. Liam was both surprised and impressed that she was able to ready her horse by herself and so easily. The palomino stood still as she moved about.

"Yer horse fits ye," Liam said as he reached out, but withdrew his hand quickly when it tried to nip him.

"He doesnae like competition for ma attention. *Vinr* is a bit temperamental around people, but he isnae troublesome with other horses. I hope ye can say the same for *Segrr*."

Liam checked theatrically to make sure he kept all his fingers.

"And ye named him Friend why? He doesnae seem particularly friendly."

"I was there at his birth, and he looked like he was going to be vera small. None of ma brothers wanted him fearing that he wouldnae grow to be a warhorse. They were going to sell him, but I convinced ma father to let me have him. He was ma only friend at the time," she shrugged, "so the name fit. Ma brother, Hamish, did help me train him. Hamish and I got along, we still do really, because he wasna too busy yet with training and ma other brothers. He taught me to tack and mount on ma own. It was his only condition to me riding with him. I didna understand then, but I do now. He wanted to be sure I could completely care for *Vinr*, so I would never be stranded somewhere, and I would be able to prove he really was ma horse if ever ma father or brothers wanted him."

Liam stood silently as he took in all the information Kyla shared. It was the most she said about her family since their first encounter in the Great Hall the day she arrived.

On their first outing on horseback, she rode close to him as he showed her the path, warning her of rabbit holes and pointing out hidden bogs. Liam realized that not only did she listen attentively, but she possessed a keen memory because, when she issued a challenge to race back to the keep, she avoided the various hazards and took daring jumps only a person who spent long hours on horseback would dare. When they returned to the stables, he pulled her from her horse and ordered all the stable workers out. He stalked her into a stall, swung the door shut behind them, and launched himself at her. She met him with equal measure, her ardor as passionate as his. He held her against him as he ravished her mouth. He pressed his tongue into her mouth, and she sucked on it until he groaned. He lowered her to the pile of fresh hay and covered her body with his before pulling up her skirts, so he could run his hand up and down the outside of her leg.

"Were ye trying to scare the life out of me or was that just an extra bit of fun? I ought to skelp yer pretty little arse," he growled into her neck. His kisses alternated with licks and nips.

Kyla tilted her head back and then to the side to give him better access. His large hand covered her breast, and much the same as with her backside, he was beyond pleased to find he had to spread his fingers as far apart as he could to support her firm, round mound. He desperately wanted to unlace her kirtle and feast upon her, but it would be much easier and faster to pull down her skirts if someone approached than trying to right the top part of her gown. He settled for running his hands over them and dipping his finger below the neckline.

"I dinna mean to scare ye. I thought it would be fun. I havenae been out for a ride since I arrived nearly a fortnight ago. I used to be able to go for a ride most afternoons. I miss being on *Vinr* and having the freedom to just ride."

Liam continued to kiss her until what she said registered.

"What do ye mean 'the freedom to just ride'? Didna anyone tell ye how far from the keep ye could go or nae go? Didna any of the guardsmen accompany ye? Yer—" He stopped before asking about her brothers.

Her arms fell to her sides, but she quickly placed them on his forearms.

"We ken nae one was overly concerned aboot where I rode as long as I was back in time to do ma chores and to ensure meals were served on time. Liam, nae everything must be taken as a personal insult on ma behalf. Neither ye nor I can change the past, so I'd rather enjoy the present and mayhap even daydream a bit aboot the future."

She grinned up at him and waggled her eyebrows.

"Cheeky," he nibbled at her lower lip before licking them.

Kyla ran her fingers through his hair and then up and down his back. Liam's fingers explored the thatch of hair at the juncture of her thighs. He dipped a finger inside of her sheath and then pulled it back out.

"Do ye ken how much I want to taste yer honey? Ye said I was like a bear that got his paw stung for dipping it in the hive. If that honey were as sweet as yers, I dinna blame him." He licked his finger. "Kyla, I want to show ye another way men and women can pleasure one another, but if ye dinna like it, ye need only tell me, and I will stop."

He watched her slowly nod her head as her eyes shifted down to his sporran. He knew she was thinking about what lay behind it. They managed only a few chances to slip away over the fortnight since her arrival. They stole kisses when they could but nothing as intimate as by the rocks or in the alley. They were both beginning to get frustrated at their lack of time alone together.

He leaned back on his heels and watched her as he slowly lifted her skirts to her waist. He kissed the inside of each of her knees then fluttered kisses up and down the inside of each thigh before kissing the nest of dark curls. He had been nearly bursting with curiosity to learn whether her hair there would be as dark as the tresses now strewn across the hay. He watched her as he blew cool air across her inflamed skin. Her hips bucked, and he caught her backside in each hand. He brought his nose to her and inhaled, groaning as he tried to slow himself. He did not want to frighten her. He slowly ran his tongue along her entrance. He traced a finger over the skin he laved and slid a finger into her. She propped herself on her elbows to see better, but she did not try to stop him. Encouraged by her interest, he pressed his tongue deeper into her and added a second finger. He ran his tongue back and forth as his fingers stroked within her. When her hips began to rock on their own accord, he sucked the sensitive button hidden with the folds. She threw back her head and arched her back. He could no longer see her face, but he knew she was biting her lip to keep from moaning too loudly. He worked her heated flesh alternating speed and pressure until he felt the spasms begin to grip his fingers. He sucked as hard as he dared, and she exploded around him. He lapped up her honey like a starving man's first meal. When she lowered herself down to the hay, he quickly pulled down her skirts and brought his body over hers.

Kyla lay with her head to the side and eyes closed. Liam saw her chest heaving as she struggled to catch her breath. He tentatively pulled hair from her damp neck and blew lightly on her overheated skin. The light breeze stirred her, and before Liam knew what was happening, he found himself flipped onto his back with Kyla laying across him. He could not believe that someone as tiny as her could move him so easily without him anticipating it. She lowered her mouth to his and licked his lips when her tongue met his, she pulled back. Liam was not sure what to make of her expression. It was a moment of surprise, distaste, and then acceptance as she dove back down to kiss him again. She growled as she pushed her hips up high enough, so she could move his sporran out of the way. When she came back down flush to him, he grasped her backside and rocked her against his iron rod. He ached to thrust inside of her. He wanted so badly to know what it felt like for them to join and become one. His body craved the physical release, but his heart's and his mind's longing for a deeper connection was far stronger.

Kyla had climaxed only moments ago, and it was the most powerful one yet, but as her still sensitive skin rubbed against the fabric of her gown which rubbed against Liam's hard body and her desire grew again, she thought about how it was always Liam pleasuring her, and she was yet to do more than merely be there. She shifted her weight to one side and slid her hand beneath his plaid. She quickly found what she was searching for and wrapped her hand around him. Her fingers barely met, and he was even longer than she anticipated. She was fascinated with how the hot, smooth skin could cover something that felt like chiseled steel below the surface.

Liam could not help the groan that came from his throat when he felt Kyla's hand wrap around him. He took several deep calming breaths before he embarrassed himself. He did not want her first attempt at pleasuring him to end abruptly before it even began.

"I dinna ken what to do."

Liam could barely hear her whisper over the pounding of his pulse in his ears. He covered her hand with his and showed her how to stroke him with a rhythm that almost made him stop her. He was too close too soon. She picked up on what he liked and began to explore. She tried holding tighter then lighter, but when she added a twist to her wrist, she felt a small trickle of fluid spill onto her thumb.

If he thought I tasted like honey, I wonder what he tastes like. Can I do that? Is it allowed for a woman to do such a thing as what he did to me? I dinna really care if it's allowed or nae. I want to ken.

Kyla was already laying between Liam's legs, so she quickly tossed his plaid up high enough to land on his face, and then swirled her tongue over the small opening she saw. She was rewarded with another trickle of fluid which she licked up. She ran her tongue from root to tip and quickly found where he was most sensitive.

Liam pushed his plaid out of the way and stared down at the woman who was taking him into her mouth. He could not believe what he saw. He never imagined she would volunteer such a thing, at least not yet, and he never planned to ask, but he could not prevent his hips from rocking forward a little. He was careful not to frighten her or overwhelm her. He watched as she closed her eyes and found her own rhythm moving up and down. What she could not manage, she stroked with her hand. Liam was on the verge of losing control when he felt her suck on him. He tried to press on her shoulders to get her to let go, but she slapped his hands away.

"Kyla, I'm too close." He tried again to push her off, but she simply tightened her lips around him.

"Kyla, ye need to stop. I'm too close. I canna, oh God, dinna stop. Feels so good. So good," Liam felt his seed squirt into the back of her throat, and she lapped it up. He was completely mortified by what he did, and words of apology were on his lips until he sat up to see that she looked like the kitten that got into the cream. She was licking her lips and smiling at him. She launched herself at him and gave him a smacking kiss.

"I finally did it!"

"Finally did what?"

"Pleasured ye the same as ye have me."

"Lass, ye didna have to do that because of what I have done for ye. I dinna expect ye to do aught but enjoy our time together."

"Liam, I did enjoy that, and I wanted to do it. I was curious to see if I would think ye taste as good as ye claim I do."

"But mo leannan, I shouldnae have let maself finish like that. A mon doesnae do that to his wife."

"Well, good thing I amnae yer wife yet. And I thought ye said whatever we do together is between us as long as we both agree and enjoy it. I think we both enjoyed that. Canna we agree on that? As for a mon nae doing that to his wife, that doesnae make sense to me. If men enjoy it, and I'm assuming they do since ye did, why would they want to stop receiving that because they are married? Wouldnae they want it more once they ken they have someone to do that with regularly?"

Liam could only look at her through a daze. His head was spinning. Each time he came together with her, his release was stronger and better, but her questioning now was also reasonable and logical. He could not clear his head enough to answer intelligently.

"But, but, it just isnae what a mon asks his lady wife to do." The moment the words came out of his mouth, he snapped it shut.

Shite! Fuck! Shite! Why couldnae I have simply stopped while I was ahead. I should have said I liked it and mayhap even thank ye.

He saw the crestfallen look on her face as she pushed away from him. She spun around and tried to right her kirtle while brushing the hay from her gown and hair.

"Kyla, wait."

"Nay. I am exactly what I was warned nae to be. I am nay better than a whore."

Liam spun her around and glared down at her.

"Dinna ever say that aboot yerself again. Ever. I dinna think that aboot ye and nay one but me kens what we do together. Nay one's opinion of what ye do with me behind closed doors," he waved his arm around, "or closed stalls, behind rocks, or between buildings matters. Dinna ever degrade yerself by thinking like that. I dinna like it. It breaks ma heart to think some auld biddy planted such doubt in yer mind and watered it long enough to take root. What I said had naught to do with ye or a judgment against ye. It was me feeling guilty for being an arse. I worried that I mistreated ye, that I dishonored ye."

"But that makes nay sense. Ye could only dishonor me if that was something only whores are supposed to do. If it is, and I did it, then I am nay better than a whore."

"*Fucking shite!*" Liam had not even realized he said those words aloud until he heard Kyla's gasp. "*Fuck! Danmit. Oh hell.*"

Liam ran his hands through his hair until it stood on end then stood with his arms akimbo.

"Why do ye even let me speak? Ever? I havenae only put ma foot in ma mouth, I've jammed them both in with ma boots on."

Kyla could not stop the giggle that welled up within her. It escaped in peals of laughter that doubled her over.

"I dinna see what's so funny. Since I amnae laughing, I ken ye are nae doing it with me but at me." He grumbled.

"Oh, mo chaileag, and ye are quite sweet," she winked at him, "I canna stay angry or even hurt when I see ye in such a twitch. Mayhap I should let ye just keep gabbing as I need a good laugh now and again." She waggled her finger for him to come closer.

When Liam bent over, she cupped his ear as if to whisper a secret.

"If ye dinna think badly of me, and ye enjoyed it, then I dinna mind doing it again as I quite enjoyed it." She lowered her hands, gave him a quick peck on the cheek, and dashed out of the stall.

Liam easily caught up with her and gave her a playful slap on her bottom before pulling a few more pieces of hay from her hair. They walked out hand in hand.

Their rides after that day were usually filled with races and rewards.

CHAPTER SIX

While Liam and Kyla continued to get to know one another better during that first fortnight of walks, rides, visits to the village, and meals spent together, there was one person at the keep who refused to share in the excitement of the new couple's growing fondness for one another.

Randall spent the first three days following his confrontation with Liam confined to his chamber. With a broken jaw and nose, and two black eyes from the punch and the broken nose, he was in too much pain to leave, which only made his mood fouler. Instead of missing time spent with his family or even time in the lists, it was his lost opportunity to find willing serving girls to soothe his many aches and pains that angered him. He was not a patient man, and he was not a man used to being denied what he wanted. In the two sennights that followed his injuries, Randall continued to stew over what he believed was an unwarranted attack by his cousin. After all, how was he supposed to know the chit was his cousin's betrothed, and even if she was, what did it matter? It would not have been the first time he shared a woman with another man. Every time he bedded a serving girl, a tavern wench, or a whore, he figured he was sharing a woman with other men. The longer he remained in self-imposed isolation, the more resentful he became. He did not want anyone to see his face, not because he was ashamed of his actions that led to the disfigurations, instead he was too vain to have any of the women who might be willing to bed him see him in such a state.

Even his parents, who usually indulged him in most things, were not sympathetic to his plight this time. His father whittled on about how they might have to leave after the incident. He kept asking aloud what would they do when they could have been living high off the hog on someone else's accounts. His mother flapped on about how he embarrassed her in front of her family, and she knew people were gossiping about them. She complained she could barely show her face around people she spent the first half of her life with because he caused such a scene. Neither of them directly stated his lust and sense of entitlement were the cause of their hardships, but it was the closest they ever came.

Once the bruising around his eyes began to fade, and the swelling of his nose lessened, Randall finally felt ready to make an appearance again. However, he was barely able to eat more than pottage with the softest of vegetables because he only recently regained enough movement in his jaw to chew and to speak intelligibly.

His first morning in the Great Hall was less than he hoped for but better than he could have expected. No one paid him any attention. While there was no talking behind hands or knowing looks, there was no sympathy offered either. Even his own guardsmen, who usually sided with him for their own well-being, said little more than a formal greeting. They could not move away when he sat down at their table, but they did nothing to include him in the conversation which became subdued when he arrived. After one mug of ale, Randall walked to the dais. By now, most of the family found their seats at the table, and there was only one unoccupied seat which was at the far end. Randall silently fumed at what he perceived as yet another slight against him when he really did nothing wrong.

That bastard has kept me shut away like a fucking leper all because I appreciated that bitch's tits. It isnae as though I didna notice aught that every other mon with a working cock doesnae see too. I'm sure I amnae the only one who wants to plow her fields, so I dinna ken why he got so upset with me. They shouldnae side with him when I'm the real victim here. I willna be humiliated and let this go.

Randall watched and waited for another sennight as his jaw continued to heal. He watched as Kyla moved through the keep charming everyone and ingratiating herself with his aunt and uncle.

Conniving wench. She isnae aught but a wolf in sheep's clothing. If she was that much of a prize, then why did her family dump her here? I ken her uncle ran off the vera next morn after bringing her here. Chased off for nae paying his bill at the tavern and nae paying for the two whores he tupped. If she was that bluidy special, why didna her father or even her brothers bring her? Instead, her lout of an uncle was the one assigned to getting rid of her.

Randall watched as Liam returned every day for the noon meal, and then they disappeared together for the entire afternoon.

As though it isnae obvious to everyone that he's already sliding between her thighs. He's surely tupping her every time they run off together. But nay, nay one says a word about the laird's soon-to-be slut by marriage. If she's spreading her legs for Liam, and they arenae married, then she isnae the moral virgin she portrays. What is good for one gander, is good for another.

Kyla was unaware she was being scrutinized so closely. Randall continued to make her uncomfortable with his brooding and glares from across the dais, but she did not give him much consideration the rest of the day.

She finished working with Arabella on the tapestry that was nearly complete. They shared a large stack of mending together, and Kyla offered to return the bedding and linens to Hagatha, the head of household. She was making her way down the back stairway when she sensed she was not alone. She stopped and looked over her shoulder, but she was walking away from the shadows, so she could not see anything but blackness behind her. She waited, but when nothing moved or appeared, she continued down the stairs. She was nearly halfway down when a hand grabbed her elbow. It yanked her back before another hand grabbed the other elbow. She was dragged back up to the top of the stairs while sheets and lines were strewn along the way. When she was able to regain her footing, she tried to twist away from her captor. A rough hand came from behind her, spinning her around, and latched painfully onto her breast. Kyla came face to face with Randall. There was a wall sconce close enough for her to see the gleam of malice in his eyes. He spun her back around.

"It's yer fault. It's all yer fault. What do ye do that has Liam so charmed? Are ye sucking his cock? Is he tossing yer skirts and playing between yer thighs. Mayhap he should learn to share. Selfish bastard," he whispered into her ear. "I'm going to start by taking ye from behind like I have been dreaming of since that first night ye flaunted these lovely tits."

Kyla felt her gown suddenly go slack from having the laces sliced, and then a dirk was beneath her chin. She did not dare move except to slowly move her hand to the secret pocket in her skirts. She slid her fingers in until she was sure her own dirk was there. Before she could pull it out, Randall yanked her gown to her waist and pinched her breast mercilessly. She struggled not to cry out in pain because she would not give him that satisfaction.

Randall made the mistake of lowering his knife to pull up his plaid as his other hand gathered up her skirts.

Kyla spun around and raised her knee, but Randall was quicker and larger. He thrust his fist into her ribs. Kyla could not help but double over. He shoved her to the ground.

"Like it rough, do ye. I'm happy to oblige."

He landed on top of her and pulled her hands over her head, pinning them in one hand. The other found her nipple and gave it an excruciating twist while he bit the soft flesh of her other breast.

Kyla folded one hand at the wrist, so her fingers came down over the tender skin between his thumb and forefinger. She pinched then dug her nails in.

Randall yelped and released her hands only to put his hand around her throat. As he pushed her skirts up, he only succeeded in bringing her pocket closer. Hands free, she used one to grab her dirk and the other to gouge at an eye. She brought both knees up between his legs at the same time slashing his side. He howled in pain and rolled off her. She wasted no time and fled the passageway, running up to her chamber where she locked and bolted the door.

She pulled the ruined gown off and searched for somewhere she could hide it until she could mend it. She folded it, hiding the severed laces as best she could, and placed it at the bottom of her chest. Kyla hissed as she twisted to see the large bruise already forming on her ribs and looked down to see the bruising and bite marks that covered her breasts. Then she moved to the small looking glass and could see bruises forming towards the back of her neck. She let down her hair and quickly ran a comb through it.

Liam willna notice if ma hair is down. Oh God, Liam. He canna find out. He will kill Randall.

Kyla rushed to pull on a chemise, but her arms hurt to stretch them over her head. She chose a kirtle that laced on the sides, so she would not have to ask for help. She checked the looking glass once more before opening her door. She looked down the passageway but could not see anyone. She dashed for the main stairway, and despite being winded from not being able to breathe deeply, she ran down the stairs until she was midway down the last flight above the Great Hall. She paused to catch her breath and to calm her racing heart. She wiped her clammy palms on her skirts and tried running her tongue around her dry mouth.

Liam was just entering the Great Hall as she reached the bottom of the steps.

He smiled warmly but then frowned. As he reached for her hand, he looked over her gown.

Bluidy hell. He's noticed.

"Is that a different gown than from earlier?"

"Aye, I noticed the other one needed mending."

There. That wasna a lie.

Kyla accepted Liam's hand and steered them towards the dais. She scanned the Great Hall to see if Randall was present. When she could not see him, she caught herself before giving an audible sigh.

The noon meal progressed without incident, and Liam suggested a walk by the loch afterward. Kyla was glad to get away from the keep. They made their way down to the loch and walked as far as they could on one side.

"Tomorrow I will take ye down to the beach if ye like. I ken I havenae taken ye there, but it's only over that ridge," he pointed out.

"That would be lovely. Mayhap one of these days I'll go for a dip."

"Ye ken that's the North Sea? There arenae many people who willingly go for a 'dip'."

"I've been swimming in the North Sea and the Minch. Aye, there's a bit of a chill, but when isnae there one in Scotland?" She shrugged her shoulders and moved closer to the shore.

She picked up a handful of stones and sorted through them. She found a couple of good ones and skipped them across the water. Liam came up behind her and slid his arms around her. She tried not to wince as his arm pressed against her sore side. When he leaned down to nuzzle her neck, she spun around, cupped his jaw, and pulled him in for a kiss.

When they finally came up for air, Liam grinned.

"I rather like this side of ye," he tapped her bottom, "and this side. I havenae found a side I didna like."

He kissed her again, and it did not take long for their kisses to grow passionate. Liam's hands traveled up and down her back. When she placed her hands on his chest, he backed them to a nearby tree, capturing them and raising them over her head. A moment of panic washed over her as memories of being held that way barely over an hour ago flooded in. She opened her eyes and looked at Liam. The fear ebbed away quickly as she looked into the familiar whisky-colored eyes. She noticed his eyes sometimes held flecks of amber in them. It was usually during moments of passion like this that made them appear. She focused on the flecks until she felt calm. She was so intent upon his eyes she did not notice when he undid the laces on both sides of her gown. She felt the neckline sag and Liam's hand upon her breast. He had never touched her like this before. If the bruising were not so fresh, she would have reveled in the sensation of him finally holding her breast that ached over and over for his touch.

Instead, the pain was so intense she could not help but suck in a gasp of air. Liam immediately pulled back.

"If ye arenae ready or dinna want me to touch ye like that, dinna be afraid to tell me. I willna ever do aught ye dinna want. "

After her traumatic experience that morning, Liam's words made her want to sob, but instead, she nodded her head.

As Liam reached out to right Kyla's gown, he noticed a mark on the top of her breast. He looked up at her and saw panic rising within her.

"Kyla, what happened to ye?"

She could not find her voice around the lump in her throat. She could only shake her head. She tried to pull the dress up, but Liam's gentle touch stayed her. He lifted her hand and kissed each finger before placing it on his heart. With his other hand, he touched the neckline of her gown. He looked up at her and waited. When she finally nodded her head, he pulled the gown down until it met her arm which she wrapped around her middle.

The sight that met Liam's eyes was something he would have nightmares about for years.

There were livid bruises all over her breasts that were clearly brand new. He could see fingerprints and bite marks. He ran his fingers above her breast but did not dare to actually touch her skin. He looked down further and saw the top of another bruise. He tried to move her arm away, so he could see more of her side, but she would not budge.

"Kyla," he warned.

She lowered her arm, and the kirtle fell to her hips.

"Holy shite," he whispered. There was a bruise that covered the entire front of her left rib cage.

He slowly walked behind her and saw the remnants of much older bruises. Liam struggled to keep himself from retching when he saw what she had suffered. Those bruises were so close to healing they could have only happened before she arrived at Dunbeath. He walked back around her.

Randall. I will fucking kill him. I will take great satisfaction in killing him with ma bare hands. Dinna even want a dirk. Ma bare bluidy hands.

"He didna rape me. I got away." Kyla whispered.

Liam saw a different kind of fear now. It was not the panic from before. It was fear mixed with shame.

"I wouldnae set ye aside. I will never set ye aside. Ye have to ken that." He stroked her cheek, but bruises on her neck caught his eye. He lifted her hair and saw finger marks on her neck. He dropped her hair and looked her in the eye.

"Who?" His voice was barely more than a whisper.

It might have sounded soft, but there was an edge of steel as rigid as a broadsword. This scared her more than any of his bellowing. She bit her lower lip. He gently pulled it loose before asking her again.

"Who, Kyla?"

A tear began to dribble from her eyes. He pulled her in for

the gentlest embrace he could. He made sure her chest did not bump his, but she tightened her hold and left no space between them. She sobbed into his chest.

"Kyla, lass, I ken ye probably dinna want to, but I must ken what happened. How did Randall attack ye?"

She leaned back to look up at him.

"Ye ken?"

"There isnae a mon in this clan that would do this to a woman, and there isnae another mon within a hundred leagues stupid enough or arrogant enough to touch ma betrothed and think there wouldnae be consequences."

"I'd finished sewing with yer mother and was using the back stairs to take the linens to Hagatha. I thought I sensed someone behind me, but when I looked, I couldnae see aught. I started back down when two hands grabbed ma arms and dragged me back. Randall said he should be able to have a turn if ye were already bedding me. When he lowered his dirk from ma neck I tried to break free. He caught me, and we landed on the ground. When I got ma hands free, I gouged his eyes, sliced him with ma own dirk, and brought ma knees to his bullocks. I ran to ma chamber and got changed before I took the main stairs to the Great Hall."

"He held a dirk to ye?"

Liam was shaking with anger. He stepped back from her and placed his hands on the sides of her shoulders.

"Use the postern gate, go to ma chamber, lock and bar the door. Dinna open it for anyone but me, nae even ma parents."

"Liam, ye're scaring me."

"*Go. Now.*" His voice was once again deadly soft.

She knew she would not dissuade him, so all she could do was nod her head. He walked her back up the hill. When he saw she made it through the gate safely, he went to the barracks. He found his second, Kenneth, and ordered him to stand guard in front of his door. When Liam told him he would kill him if he allowed anyone in, Kenneth was wise enough not to ask questions.

They walked to the Great Hall together in silence. Once Liam saw Kenneth climbing the stairs, he turned to the dais. Randall made an appearance after the meal was done. He sat to the side while their parents continued to talk to one another. Liam's vision once again tunneled, and everything but Randall faded to black. He felt the same battle lust course through him that saved him countless times over the ten years spent going into battle.

Liam pulled one of his dirks loose and launched it towards Randall. He ensured it landed in the wood right over his shoulder. The room became silent immediately, so Liam's voice carried even though he spoke softly.

"Dinna think I missed. I was giving ye fair warning."

He stalked towards the dais and leaped up. He pulled Randall from his chair, and in a feat that would later surprise even him, lifted the man over his head before throwing him to the ground. He jumped down and pulled Randall to his feet. He pulled another dirk from his waist and brought it to Randall's throat and pressed hard enough to draw a trickle of blood.

"I warned ye nae to say another word aboot her, and instead ye touched her. Ye put yer hands on her. I will kill ye. Ye maynae have raped her," Liam was sure to say the last part loudly enough to satisfy any of the gossips. "But ye still touched her."

"She asked for it. She wanted it. Now she's blaming me. She's naught more than a harlot."

"Nae woman asks for the bruises and marks ye left on her. That wasna by choice. Ye maynae have succeeded, but ye tried to rape her. Yer eye looked much better this morn, but now there is a fresh bruise. I wonder why." Liam sliced open both sides of Randall's leine to show a bandage with fresh blood on it. "I didna do that, and ye havenae been in the lists. Who would have done that but someone trying to defend themselves. I will kill ye."

Liam raised his voice before going on.

"Let this be a lesson to anyone who might think of touching what is mine. She will always come first."

He sensed movement behind him. Before his father could say anything, he ground out, "If Mama doesnae want blood on her fresh rushes, I challenge this pile of pig shite to single combat, but it will be to the death. I willna settle for less."

"Son, ye are within yer rights." Donnell turned to look over his shoulder at his sister and brother by marriage. "I'm sorry, but he brought this upon himself."

The MacDougall was not convinced.

"Ye dinna ken for sure. The chit may be lying. Liam caught her after she'd been with someone else, and she blamed Randall to escape Liam's wrath."

Liam's roar of fury rivaled any battle call.

"Open yer eyes, ye blathering eejit. Hasnae it ever crossed either of yer minds that an unusually large number of bairns born to yer unwed serving lasses bear a striking resemblance to either side of yer family? It's nae great secret he's sired bastards from here to Argyllshire. Do ye really believe his prowess is so great that every single one of those women clamored to be in his bed? Uncle, ye ken how Randall told ye he was robbed by highwaymen after selling last year's whisky? There were nay highwaymen. He pissed it all away gambling or rather paying off his gambling debts. Aunt Ellen, do ye ken how ma grandmother's jewels went missing from yer chamber and ye thought one of the serving lasses took it? The lass was lashed because Randall named her as the thief. Randall took yer jewels before he left to sell the whisky. He used them to gamble with on the way, and then because of those debts, he used the whisky money to pay them off."

Liam could hear his aunt's soft cries from behind, and while he felt remorse for being the cause of her tears, he felt no guilt over spilling Randall's secrets. He was to inherit the lairdship from his father, and it would only be a matter of time before he ruined their clan.

He heard his uncle's sigh before hearing his resignation.

"Son, ye have brought this upon yerself. There isnae aught I can do when a mon rightfully demands single combat."

Liam pulled his dirk from Randall's neck and pushed him towards the massive double doors. Once they were off the steps, Randall whipped around as he drew his sword, but Liam was already ready. He pulled his double-handed broadsword from its sheath, and after years of training, he was able to use only one hand to maneuver the sword, so he kept the dirk in the other. The sword was twice the width and almost twice the weight of his cousin's regular broadsword. Liam took one swing to gain him time to get into the position he wanted. Randall lunged forward again, aiming for Liam's midsection, but it was an easy strike to block with Liam's wider sword.

"She wrapped her lips around ma cock like an Edinburgh whore. Ye've trained her well, Cousin." Randall taunted Liam, and when he did not receive a response from Liam, he tried again.

"Naught to say in her defense? Those beautiful thighs opened for me, and she gave me a good ride."

Liam heard Randall's jeers and taunts but refused to respond. Instead, he focused entirely on Randall's sword and the man's movements. He let the words float past him as he continued to engage Randall in the fight. Liam knew he was the superior swordsman, and he was already easily wearing the other man down. Randall was beginning to tire from trying to speak and fight at the same time. They danced back and forth while Randall was still on the offense. His opening came sooner than he expected when Randall raised his arm to swipe downwards, intending to cleave Liam in half. Liam kept his massive sword in one hand and thrust forward with the dirk in his other hand. The dirk found its mark as it embedded between Randall's ribs. The man stumbled backward from the force, the surprise, and the immediate pain. Liam followed him with a series of punishing sword strikes that shredded Randall's sword arm, sliced into the other set of ribs, and finally plunged into his chest. Randall collapsed like a rag doll landing in a heap in the dirt.

Liam wiped away the sweat from his brow and stood over his dying cousin.

"I gave ye fair warning." He looked up towards the crowd that surrounded them. "I give ye all a fair warning. Dinna ever touch what is mine. She is mine, and I will always defend her. I dinna care who it is. I dinna care which clan they are from. The papers have been signed that bind us together. She is ma wife by arrangement and by choice. Nae one will harm her and live." He spat on Randall as he pulled his sword free. As the last breath left the man's body and his eyes dimmed, Liam wiped his sword clean. Then he looked up again at the crowd.

"This mon said many untrue things about Lady Kyla. If there is anyone here who believed him, step forward now, and we will settle this. I willna have anyone question her honor, nae now, nae once she is Lady Sinclair."

His demand was met with silence until the most unlikely woman stepped forward.

"Ma lord," Bethea pushed her way forward through the crowd. When she came to stand in front of Liam, she surprised not only Liam but the entire clan. "I dinna think there is one among us who believed what that sod said. Nae only have we come to ken Lady Kyla and ken she isnae a loose woman, we like her vera much. She is kind to all and works harder than most. But more importantly than that, it is obvious to all and sundry how much ye care for each other. It isnae possible that she would choose to stray from ye. If the situation were switched, I wouldnae put it past the lass to heave that hulking sword of yers at anyone who disparaged ye."

It took a moment for the clan to overcome their shock that Bethea would defend anyone, especially an outsider, but once they had, there was vigorous agreement. The crowd cheered on Liam, and many voices could be heard raised in support of Kyla. Liam looked around his clan, proud of his people for seeing past the evil words that were flung about that day and proud of the woman who he could not wait to see.

"Thank ye all. It makes ma heart happy to hear yer support." Liam sheathed his sword and made his way through the crowd as many clapped him on the back. He paused only in front of his parents who stood next to his aunt and uncle. He looked at his father who only nodded his head. He looked to his aunt and uncle and saw sadness, but also anger. He wished he could say something of comfort or remorse, but he had nothing. He made his way into the keep with only one destination in mind.

CHAPTER SEVEN

Liam made his way above stairs and nodded to Kenneth when he reached his door. He knocked on the door "Lass, it's me. Open the door, please. "

He barely finished speaking before the door flung open and a soft blur hurtled towards him. He caught Kyla as she pressed her mouth to his. Her kiss was desperate and seeking. Liam held her as he stepped into the chamber and kicked the door shut. Kyla did not ease off in her kiss. She slid her tongue along his lips and plunged it into his mouth the moment Liam opened enough for it to slide in. As they explored one another's mouths, Kyla's arms searched every part of Liam's body she could reach. Unable to see clearly, she grappled with the brooch on his shoulder.

"Down," she panted.

Liam set her down and began to pull away. Kyla's hand shot up and yanked on his leine to keep him kissing her. She fiddled first with his sporran to drop his brooch into it, and then with the belt that kept his plaid in place. She growled when she could not release the prong. Liam's hands covered hers until it sprung loose. As the belt gave way, Kyla felt cool air waft against her sides and then her breasts. She caught Liam's plaid as it began to fall. She flung it behind her assuming it would land on the nearby chair. She pulled her arms loose of her own sleeves as he pulled her kirtle down past her hips. She yanked up on his leine as high as she could reach. He pulled it over his head and let it drop to the floor next to his sporran and belt. He grasped the front of her chemise and tore it open. That too landed on the floor. He yanked off his boots as she rolled down her stockings and slipped off her slippers. Kyla moaned, and Liam growled as their bare bodies finally came into full contact with one another.

Liam scooped Kyla into his arms and walked to the bed, their kiss unbroken. He lowered her to the bed, but instead of climbing over her, he laid on his side next to her. When she reached for him, he caught her hand and kissed her palm. Then he feathered his fingers over her bruised chest.

"I willna, I canna, do this unless ye are ma wife. I willna take advantage of ye."

Kyla's brow furrowed.

"Are ye worried ye might get me with child before we are wed? I'm sure a few days or even a couple of weeks would go unnoticed."

"That isnae it."

"Are ye worried if ye discover I amnae a maiden before we are wed, ye'll have to set me aside?"

"Nay! I will *never* set ye aside. I will never consider that. It hasnae aught to do with that. I believe ye when ye said he didna do *that*. And I kenned already ye are a maiden, nae that that would stop me from wedding ye."

When Kyla looked confused, Liam explained, "We maynae have coupled yet, but I have felt yer maidenhead."

Kyla nodded her head slowly as Liam watched her mind tick over.

"Havenae ye always said it's ma choice about what I want to or dinna want to do?"

"Aye, but--"

"Are ye taking that back now? Instead of ever forcing me, ye would deny me?

"Kyla, I love ye. I want to ken that the first time, every time, we make love, we are completely joined. Nae just in body. I dinna want to do this until I have pledged myself to ye in thought, word, and deed."

"Ye love me? Liam, I love ye too. That's precisely why I dinna want to wait. I want to offer to ye something I willna ever give to anyone else. I already have given ye ma heart and soul. Now I would give ye ma body, so we might be one."

They entwined fingers and looked at each other. Liam felt himself drowning in the depth of her blue eyes. Kyla drank in the whisky brown windows to his soul.

"I love ye, sgaoileadh," whispered Kyla. *My heart.*

"I love ye, m'anam," whispered Liam. *My soulmate.*

Looking into one another's eyes, they both seemed to come to the same realization at the same moment.

"Handfast," they said together.

"Aye, mo leannan." Liam smiled broadly.

"Right now," she responded.

Kyla rolled onto her side, so they faced one another. Liam brushed her hair back over her shoulder. Kyla placed one of his hands over her heart, then placed one of hers over his heart, and held his free hand.

"I take ye ma heart at the rising of the moon, and the setting of the stars. To love and to honor through all that may come. Through all our lives together, in all our lives, may we be reborn that we may meet and ken and love again and remember." Liam pledged.

"I swear by peace and love to stand, heart to heart and hand to hand. Mark, O Spirit. And hear me now, confirming this ma Sacred vow." Kyla vowed.

Together they made their final pledge.

"Ye are blood of ma blood, and bone of ma bone. I give ye ma body, that we two might be one. I give ye ma spirit, 'til our life shall be done. To thee, I do pledge ma troth."

Their kiss was softly filled with love and devotion. Keeping their hands over one another's hearts, they watched each other while their other hand began to explore. Kyla ran her hands down over the rungs of his stomach, fascinated with how the muscles quivered as she touched them. She ran her hand over his hip finding a groove that seemed to have been made only for her. Liam slowly ran his fingertips along the inside of her thigh and ran them through the thatch at her hips. Kyla rolled onto her back and let her knees fall open. Liam slid his fingers down to her wet entrance, and he groaned as he felt how prepared her body was for him already. Knowing this was her first time, he went slowly to draw out her pleasure and to ready her body. He knew he was a large man, and while she had broad hips, she was still half his size.

Kyla enclosed his rod with her hand and began to stroke slowly as Liam's fingers entered her. He felt himself leak slightly as his body reacted to hers. He moved his fingers and twisted to find the exact spot that brought her the most sensation as his thumb rubbed over her tender button. She arched her hips towards his seeking fingers and moaned. Liam slid down the bed despite Kyla's protest when she had to let go. He pressed her legs to open further as he breathed warm then cool then warm air over her tender folds. He laved his tongue up and down slowly before dipping it into her sheath. Kyla let out a shudder as she gripped the sheets around her. She could feel the pressure build as her core ached and tightened. Her pleasure burst forward as her inner muscles spasmed. Liam brought himself up and over her on his forearms. Before he knew what was happening, he once again found himself on his back. He watched with fascination as she slid her body down his, trailing her breasts over his heated skin. She watched him as she moved and ran her tongue slowly over her lips. When she reached her destination, she licked from stem to stern as she discovered more and more that brought him pleasure. Finally, she took as much into her mouth as she could. What she could not manage, she covered with her hand. She moved up and down as she drew her cheeks in, and her hand moved in time, adding that twist she had noticed he enjoyed. It was Liam's turn to grasp the sheets as he watched the most erotic scene he had ever experienced. When an undeniable need to rock his hips began to build, he leaned forward, lifting her up, and flipped her onto her back.

Kyla had a sensation of flying for a moment before she landed on feathers with a rock pressing onto her. She drew her ankles up and spread her knees wide. Liam kissed her with a passion that built not only over the time they were in his chamber, but the weeks spent falling in love. He eased into her, using every last bit of control he had not to thrust, and waited for her to adjust to the new feeling. Kyla wrapped her ankles over his calves and lifted her hips to meet him.

Liam raised his head to lock eyes with her. He mouthed, "I'm sorry," before taking a breath and breaking through her barrier.

"I love ye," he said as he seated himself to the hilt. She dug her nails into him as sharp pain streaked through her abdomen. He watched Kyla adjust to him.

"I love ye, too," she whispered as she shifted slightly.

Liam dropped his head and groaned.

This is better than I could have ever imagined. She's so tight she'll milk me dry if I dinna slow things. I willna finish without her. Dear Heavenly Father, thank ye for this woman. I will never forsake the blessing ye have given me. By all that's holy, I amnae going to last if she keeps kissing ma neck and sucking ma earlobe. I need to thrust, but I dinna want to hurt her. Shite! I canna stop. Feels so good.

Liam strained to maintain a slow pace, but Kyla pressed up with each of his thrusts. She found the grooves on his hips again and used them to give her more leverage. She anchored her feet to give her own thrusts more power.

"More, Liam. Harder. So good," she panted.

Dinna stop. Please, dinna stop. I need him. Finally, I ken what ma body has been missing. I finally feel full in a way his fingers and tongue couldnae give me. Sweet Jesu, I would climb into his skin if it could get me closer. I need him to keep going. Just a little bit more. So close.

"Kyla, dinna stop. Ye feel so good. What are ye doing to me? I canna stop. I dinna want to hurt ye, mo ghaol, but--"

Liam felt her inner muscles begin to clench, and he was lost. He thrust harder and faster as Kyla tilted her head back and screamed his name.

"*Liam!*"

He felt his seed piston from him as it hit her core. His own bellow followed.

"*Kyla!*"

Liam immediately wrapped her in his arms and rolled them over. He knew his arms were too spent to support him, but neither would he crush her or let her go. She clung to him as she tried to catch her breath. Her heart beat so heavily, and she was so choked up with emotion, she could hardly breathe. She listened to Liam's heart beat in tandem with her own. He lifted her heavy and damp hair from her neck and draped it across his chest. He marveled at how it shone.

"An eagle's wing."

Kyla lifted her head to look at him.

"Yer hair is like an eagle's wing. Ye are just as glorious to watch as ye soar." He grinned and winked at the end.

"Ye arenae a stung bear. Ye are a majestic red deer."

Liam puffed out his chest until her next comment made him laugh.

"Aye, vera horny."

"Antlers."

"Just as I said." She raised one eyebrow.

Liam pulled her in and kissed her temple.

"Ye have quite the saucy sense of humor. What have I unleashed? A bird of prey or mayhap a wildcat."

Kyla reached down to run her hand over his cock, and it twitched of its own volition. She ran her hand lower and cupped his bullocks as she gently rolled them in her palm. She was fascinated by all she was learning about Liam's body, and the small masculine sounds he made only excited her more. She smiled seductively when her hand wrapped around him and began to stroke his already aroused flesh.

"Wildcat," she purred.

Shocked his body was begging to go again so soon, Liam pulled her legs to straddle his hips and lifted her, so the entrance to her core glided over his engorged rod. He could feel she was as eager as he was.

"Hold on to me and guide me in."

"Like this? We can make love like this?"

"Lass, there is any number of ways to make love, but this is the one we can try now. Slowly lower yerself onto me. Dinna rush because ye may already be sore. I dinna want to hurt ye."

As she slid down and took him completely into her, she moaned. Liam tried to lift her off.

"What? Did I do aught wrong? Did I hurt ye?" she panted.

"Nay. It's the opposite. I dinna want to keep hurting ye. We dinna have to continue right now."

"Ye maynae have to, but I dinna plan to stop. Ye arenae hurting me. That was the sound of pleasure. Feeling ye enter me is almost as good as the release. I dinna ken if I will ever stop being surprised at how incredibly good it feels when we come together. Even the first time, when there was a wee pinch, the feeling of ye moving into me was better than aught I could have imagined. Dinna make us stop, Liam. I want to make love to ma husband again."

"As ye wish, ma wife. I rather like the sound of that. I can quite easily get used to that. It's as though it's as it always should be."

They moved together slowly as Kyla experimented with different movements and rhythms. Liam was sure he would go cross-eyed in his attempts to hold back long enough for Kyla to find what brought her the most pleasure.

Bluidy hell. I am going to spill again already. I havenae come to climax this fast since the first few times I took maself in ma own hand, and that was easily over ten summers ago. Nae one has ever felt this good. Naught has ever felt this good. There will never be anyone else. Nae now, nae even when we meet our maker. Lord, please dinna take her first. I dinna ken if I will survive without her. I ken I dinna want to live another day without her.

Kyla moved over Liam slowly as she found new ways to heighten their passion. She alternated rising and lowering with rocking forward and back. She swiveled her hips and found that elicited a growl and thrust for Liam. She continued moving her hips since every thrust from Liam brought her closer to her finish. They crested together in a tangle of arms and legs that seemed to have no beginning and no end.

I love this mon more than I ever could have imagined. I certainly didna think I was even going to like him after what I heard him say in the beginning. I am glad I didna run away like I considered before he turned around. I have found a mon who loves me as much as I love him. I pray we grow old together surrounded by our children and their children. I dinna ken how I will survive when he rides off to battle. I would keep him here beside me always. I dinna ken if I could make it without him. I dinna ever want to live without him again.

Liam pulled a blanket over them as he felt Kyla's skin begin to chill. She felt her eyes droop as a wave of fatigue washed over her. The day was catching up to her, and she could barely stay awake.

"Rest, ma love. I will stay with ye always. I willna leave yer side." Liam whispered as he stroked circles on her back, and she drifted off.

Liam found his own eyes growing heavy once he felt her breathing slow and become deeper. He wrapped his arms around her and fell asleep with her cocooned in his embrace.

It was nearly two hours later when they both began to stir. Kyla opened her eyes as Liam was returning to the bed with a wet linen square. He eased onto the bed and kissed her forehead.

"How do you feel, mo chridhe?"

"Well. I do feel better for having slept for a little while. I had nae realized I was so tired."

Liam nodded as he reached over to run the cloth between her legs. Kyla jumped and pushed his hand away. She was mortified to see him try to clean her, but when she looked down, she saw the remnants of the evidence of her lost maidenhead. She looked up at Liam who smiled softly. Her gaze slid down his stomach, and she noticed he must have already cleaned himself.

"Kyla, there isnae aught to be embarrassed about, nae between us." Once again, he leaned forward to kiss her forehead.

She nodded her head slowly and laid back against the pillow. She was still horrified, but she accepted his ministrations. When he was done, she felt his hand trail softly over her bruised skin. She had not noticed any of the discomforts while they were making love. He slid his arms around her, and she reached for him.

"I am sorry if I caused ye more pain or discomfort. I wasna as considerate as I should have been. I didna think about yer bruises."

"Ye didna. I mean, ye didna cause me discomfort. I was so caught up in what we were doing, what I felt with ye and about ye, I didna notice them. Ma ribs are a bit sore, but the rest dinna hurt as badly as they look."

"The healer can see ye and give ye a balm of some sort, I would think. I can call for a warm bath, so ye can soak."

"I dinna need all of that. Though a bath, later, would be nice. Will ye scrub ma back? She tickled his ribs.

"Och, aye. I'll do a fair bit more than just that." Liam grinned wolfishly.

Kyla pulled away and slid to the edge of the bed.

"We best make our way below stairs. Yer family will be wondering what has become of us."

"Ours," he said from over her shoulder, "and I amnae worried. I'm sure the entire keep kens exactly what has become of ye." He playfully spanked her backside as she stood.

Kyla flushed red as she made her way around the bed to begin finding her clothing. As she bent over to pick up her chemise, she felt Liam step behind her. As she straightened, his hands came to her hips.

"This is one of the most glorious sights in all of Scotland."

He pulled her hips back, so she could feel his arousal. When she tried to turn, he stayed her. He jutted his chin towards the looking glass that stood before them. She saw them standing there and took in the sight of their naked bodies pressed against each other. Liam towered over her and was twice as broad, but she never really considered the significance of their size difference until she saw them then. She took in his muscular hands, arms, and chest that could easily crush her but were always tender. She reached over her shoulder until Liam bent forward. She used the mirror to guide her hand as she brushed a stray lock of hair from over his eyebrow. She often wanted to do that, but she thought it was not her place to do so.

"I suppose I can do that now. Mayhap even in public from time to time."

"Brush the hair from ma face? Ye've always been able to do that. I amnae going to keep ma love or affection for ye a secret, and ye dinna have to be afraid to touch me whenever ye want."

He grinned as he slid his hands up to her breasts that stretched forward with her arm raised. He held the underside to avoid pressing on any of the bruises. Kyla was mesmerized by the sight of them in the looking glass. When she moved slightly over the back of the chair in front of them to get a clearer view, the crease of her backside rubbed against his already hard rod. She paused before moving her buttocks again. She was surprised by the arousal this created deep within her belly.

Liam could not get enough of what he saw before him. He pulled his hands back to caress the silky skin of her back and bottom. He kneaded the supple and ample flesh apart. He gazed down at her sacred rosebud and let his mind wander to a time when he might introduce her to a hidden pleasure. He slid his length against it and then through the dew between her thighs. He could not stop the groan that escaped when he felt how wet she was for him again. Her desire and arousal always matched his, and he delighted in it.

"Liam, is it supposed to feel so good when ye do that? Back there?"

"Where, lass?" He ran his finger over the small of her back and lower until he reached the sensitive skin hidden to him up until now. "Here? Or lower?"

"Both, but there. That was what I was talking aboot. Is it supposed to feel good? Is that—" She could not continue. She did not know if this was the topic that would finally be too brazen.

"It can, for both people. It is something that can take getting used to for a woman, and if it is rushed, it can cause pain. But if it's done slowly and properly, it can bring great pleasure to both."

For the second time since meeting Liam, the realization that he had been with other women overwhelmed her. There was no other way he could know this without having experienced it. She only nodded but no longer wanted to watch them in the looking glass.

"What happened? Did I scare ye? Ye're retreating from me."

She shook her head as she straightened.

"Kyla?"

She took a deep breath before answering.

"I doubt that is something ye discuss with yer friends, at

least nae like that, so the only way ye ken is because ye have done that before. And ye ken ye like it which ye probably realized after trying it more than once. I didna ever think I was the type to be jealous, but I find I am. Quite intensely jealous. If ye've even done that, then there is naught that is new to ye when it is all new to me. There isnae aught that is just mine when it is all just yers."

"I canna do aught to change what I did before I met ye. I told ye that once before. I admit there were some others in the past, but nae a great many. Ma past does mean I ken now how to please ye." Liam wanted to kick himself when the last words came out of his mouth. Kyla stiffened and tried to step away.

"Wait. That didna sound as good aloud as it did in ma head. I meant it was as though ma past was preparing me for ma life with ye. What we share is a passion unlike any I have ever imagined, and I want to always bring ye the fulfillment and pleasure I crave for ye to have. I dinna ken that I could if I hadnae some experience. But, Kyla, ye are wrong to think naught is new or naught is only yers. All of this is new to me because I have never made love before. Before it was about passing the time or finding physical release. Never have I been emotionally attached to a woman, nor have I ever wanted to be before. I certainly have never brought another woman in here. Ye are the only woman who has shared this bed. There will never, ever, be another woman in that bed till the day I meet our maker. There will never be another woman anywhere."

Kyla relaxed slightly as she took in what Liam vehemently said. She knew it would be unreasonable to hold his past against him, but it still stung.

"There is one thing I most definitely have never done with another woman. Kyla, I have never spilled ma seed within another woman, at least nae in the way that begets a bairn. I have never wanted to risk siring a bastard. That is the reason why I used this way," he ran a finger over her bottom, "when I coupled in the past. It was safer that way."

"But ye like it?"

"I only discovered that after I decided I wouldnae risk siring a bastard. Aye, I have coupled with women in the traditional sense, but once I was old enough to really understand the risk, it lost its appeal. There arenae many women who will do that." He tapped her again.

"Is that yer way of letting me ken ye havenae tupped that many women?"

"I suppose ye could say that, but it means there is much that is still new to me too."

She slowly nodded her head as she leaned back against him. He wrapped his arm around her waist as he pulled her hair away from her neck. He kissed a small trail over her shoulder, up her neck, to slightly behind her ear.

"I dinna want aught to ever hurt ye," he whispered, "I would always protect ye. I dinna want ma past to hurt ye either. I love ye and only ye. It has only ever been ye."

She turned her head to look back at him and caught his mouth in a lingering kiss. The longer it lasted, the more intense it grew.

I dinna love kenning there were other women, but there isnae aught I can do aboot it. Lingering over that isnae going to get us anywhere, at least nae a place I want to go. I love him, and I believe he loves me. It is true he has done naught since I met him to make me think otherwise. Let this go, Kyla. Let this go.

Kyla leaned forward over the back of the chair in front of her. She stood on her tiptoes and pressed her hips back. It took only a moment before Liam kissed the center of her back and slid himself into her. Liam held her around the waist as his other arm slid up between her breasts to her shoulder. He supported almost all her weight as he slowly rocked in her. She gripped the chair as a wave of new sensations washed over her from this new position. It felt as though he was reaching all the way to her core. He continued rocking them as she grew more accustomed to the heightened sensations. Liam lifted one of her legs, so her foot rested on the arm of the chair. He groaned as he pressed further, so close to meeting his release.

I canna climax until she has. I willna be that selfish. Nae ever if I can help it. I dinna want to anyway. The feel of her, the look of her when she climaxes with me will forever be seared into ma memory. Aught less would shortchange me. I dinna want to do any of this without her.

Liam slid his hand from her waist down to her enflamed folds and found the place that would heighten her pleasure. He rubbed in slow circles until she was moaning.

"Can we move faster? Can—can ye—harder. Harder, Liam."

That was all the invitation he needed. He pulled back almost all the way out before plunging into her again and again. She met each thrust with one of her own, thrusting her own hips back to meet him.

"Dear God in heaven, what are ye doing to me? Are ye close, lass? I dinna ken if I can wait much longer. I willna finish without ye."

"So close. Dinna stop aught. Merciful heavens, this is beyond what I imagined. Ye feel so hard and so big. Liam, I'm there. I— Liam!"

She could not finish her thought as his name was wrought from her very soul.

"Kyla!" Liam felt as though he was floating and watching from above. The sight of her as they made love touched him to a depth he did not know he was capable of.

They both collapsed forward as they tried to catch their breath. He slowly pulled away, but Kyla reached back to grab his hip.

"Nae yet."

"I ken. I didna want to crush ye."

They stayed joined together watching themselves in the looking glass until Liam felt Kyla shiver. He pulled away from her and lifted her into his arms. He carried her back to the bed and laid her down before covering her with a blanket. He padded softly to the door and opened it. He spotted a maid moving through the passageway and called out to her to have Hagatha send up a bath.

He reclosed the door and moved back to the bed. He froze when he saw Kyla tucked into it with her hair strewn across the pillows.

She is finally in ma bed. Our bed.

She reached for him as he climbed in beside her. Liam pulled the bed curtains closed before drawing her close and tucking her beneath his chin. It was not long before there was a knock on the door. He called out for them to enter and a troop of servants entered with the tub, buckets of steaming water, and drying linens.

"Lord Liam, would ye like me to scrub ye back," purred one of the serving girls.

Liam watched as Kyla bristled like a scalded cat. He managed to not laugh, but he did grin. She growled softly.

"Lass, I havenae needed anyone to bathe me since I was out of short strings."

"Get out the lot of ye," came Hagatha's authoritative voice.

Once the door closed, Hagatha did not wait to make it clear that they might fool others, but they were not fooling her.

"I brought yer favorite lemongrass soap and oil. I've also brought a fresh chemise and kirtle. Ye'll both be wanting to hurry up a might if ye're to make the evening meal. Nae that anyone is expecting to see ye, I suppose, but I willna be telling Elspeth to send up a tray."

With that, Liam and Kyla heard the door click again. Liam knew Hagatha was speaking the truth, and that her sister, Elspeth the cook, would not send up a tray.

Kyla felt as though her face was on fire. First from annoyance and then from mortification.

"I told ye the entire keep kens ye are well," Liam chuckled.

"Dinna tease. Mayhap ye'd rather someone else scrub yer

back. I can go back to ma own chamber."

"Dinna fash. That lass, whomever she was, hasnae bathed me nor anyone else other than Hagatha, and that was a score ago. And ye are in yer chamber."

Liam did not wait for a response before he carried her over to the tub. He climbed in and arranged her, so she straddled him. He scooped water over her shoulders and watched, fascinated, as it trickled down over and between her breasts. Kyla reached for a linen square and lathered it with soap. She began to run the linen over his shoulders and chest before traveling down the notches of his abdomen. She was intrigued by how different his body was from her own.

"Marking yer territory?" He cocked an eyebrow. "Ye ken ye dinna need to make me smell like a garden. I amnae interested in anyone but ye."

"Ye think this is for ye? Daft mon, I am marking ma territory, so nay other woman gets confused and thinks ye arenae mine. Nay one touches what's mine."

Liam found he quite liked having his own words turned on him.

They finished bathing one another with only a brief delay before Liam helped her into her kirtle. Kyla arranged her hair up in a simple chignon.

"I like yer hair down," Liam said as he kissed her neck. "Though this has definite benefits."

"If I am a married woman now, I canna be wearing ma hair down. I dinna have a kertch yet, but I will be sure to make one."

Kyla paused and looked down. With no mother of her own, there would be no one to bless her kertch, a linen triangle worn over the hair of married women, or to tie it on for the first time. Liam slid his arms around her and pulled her back flush to his chest.

"Ma mother will do it." He said softly. He kissed her temple and felt her relax. "We'd best make our way below stairs, or Hagatha will let us starve."

CHAPTER EIGHT

When the couple reached the Great Hall, the mood was subdued and somber. Tucked away in their love nest, Liam and Kyla were able to put recent events aside, but now they came crashing back in. With a hall of eyes pointed towards them, Kyla wanted to shy away, but she forced herself to be composed. She set her head high, back ramrod straight, and plastered her serene look onto her face. Liam wrapped his arm around her waist, and when she tried to step aside afraid of impropriety, he held tight mouthing the word "mine." She nodded her head and mouthed the word back. She lifted his hand and stepped away far enough to take his hand in hers. He knotted his fingers with hers as he looked down at with her with such pride that she felt like her heart might burst.

Thank the blessed Lord once again for bringing this treasure to me. Mayhap ma father did ken what he was doing. I couldnae have found anyone better suited to me. Let me continue to be worthy of her love.

Liam lifted their clasped hands and kissed her knuckles.

Heavenly Father, I have tried nae to ask for aught, or at least nae much, but ye have given with both hands. Liam is like manna from above. Let me continue to be worthy of his love.

When they looked at one another, something silent passed between them that bonded them even more than the joining of their bodies. They nodded to one another before walking to the dais.

"She would show her face here after what she did!"

Kyla's head whipped around at the sound of Liam's irate uncle. Liam pressed her behind him and took a defensive stance with his feet planted hip-width apart and arms crossed. He was easily more than half a foot taller than his uncle and at least four stones heavier. He tilted his head from side to side, and the sound of his neck cracking seemed to echo through the Great Hall.

"Tread carefully, Uncle. That *she* is ma wife now." Liam paused to let the news settle in. "Ye ken as well as I, and everyone here, this wasna her fault. Dinna even think to blame her, the victim, when it was yer son who erred. And it cost him. Aunt Ellen has been through enough, dinna leave her a widow too."

Liam's threat was clear, and he sensed his parents move to their side, but he never took his eyes from his Uncle.

"Shamus, ye ken we've had some time to learn from yer guardsmen that Liam spoke true aboot Randall. He did naught that wasna within his rights as the lass's betrothed. She's his wife now. He'll have even more grounds for recompense if ye slander her." Donnell leaned towards his brother by marriage and whispered, "Ye arenae as young as ye once were. Ye will nae survive to tell the tale. Leave off."

Arabella moved to Kyla's side and wrapped her arms around the younger woman.

"Dinna fash. Neither Donnell nor Liam will let any harm come to ye. Welcome to our family, daughter."

Kyla looked at Arabella and saw the sincerity in her warm eyes and smile. She nodded her head slightly.

"Shamus, ye and ma sister are always welcome here, but I think it best if ye leave in the morn."

Ellen stepped up to her husband and placed her hand on his arm. He yanked it away but a moment later guided her off the dais.

Once Liam was sure the older couple was above stairs, he relaxed and turned to find both his mother and father embracing Kyla. She was so petite that she looked swallowed by his mother and much larger father.

"Mama, Da," he reached for Kyla's hand, and once he could place his arm around her, he continued, "I didna wish to kill ma own cousin, but Kyla will always come first. I ken that may nae make me a good laird, but it will always be true."

"Son, that type of loyalty and fidelity is what this clan looks to in its leader. There will be times where ye will be challenged to do that, and I think yer lass is the type to understand and support ye when it seems like ye canna put her first, but remain equal partners in all, and it will forever be true." Donnell looked down at his own wife as he pulled her in for a kiss that confirmed to Kyla exactly where Liam got his charm and virility.

"So, ye're wed are ye." Arabella raised a thin eyebrow.

"Handfasted, Arabella."

"Mama, if ye are willing."

Kyla could not help but grin widely.

"And it's Da to ye, too."

Kyla nodded.

"Mama, Da, I would like Father Michael to wed us as soon as possible. This isnae for merely a year and a day."

"We assumed as much. Sunset tomorrow eve." Arabella responded.

"In the meantime," Arabella removed the kertch from her own head and stepped to Kyla. She looked to Hagatha and Elspeth who came to the dais. "We are yer kin and clan, Kyla. We welcome ye to Clan Sinclair. We might wait till after the kirk, but I dinna think ye'll be any more married tomorrow than ye already are today." She waggled both eyebrows this time and turned Kyla to face the clan members seated at the tables.

Arabella, Hagatha, and Elspeth each took a corner of the kertch and held it over Kyla's head.

"If there is righteousness in the heart, there will be beauty in the character," Arabella stated clearly.

"If there is beauty in the character, there will be harmony in the home." Hagatha recited strongly.

"If there is harmony in the home, there will be order in the clan," Elspeth spoke steadily.

"If there is order in the clan, there will be peace in the land." The women said in unison.

"So let it be!" cheered the clan.

The three women placed the kertch over Kyla's hair, and she could not stop the tears that slid down her cheeks.

"Thank ye," she managed in a hoarse whisper.

The laird's family and all the clan members settled in for the evening meal. It was uneventful compared to all that happened earlier in the day. The relative calm settled over Kyla, and she felt herself growing weary as the meal progressed. It was not long before she could barely keep her eyes open. She leaned her head against Liam's shoulder until she realized what she did. She quickly looked about the Great Hall to see if anyone noticed. Those who had simply smiled knowingly. She tried to sit up straighter but found herself suddenly perched upon the very hard and muscular lap of her husband.

Ma husband. I rather like the sound of that. I ken I dinna have aught to be jealous of, at least nae anymore, but I am glad every woman in here sees this. He picked me up and set me on his lap. Even though he smells so good even with ma soap, there is still something aboot him that is uniquely his scent.

She caught herself as she sniffed his neck. On her deep inhale, Liam looked down and smiled.

"Do ye wish to retire for the eve? I will take ye to our chamber if ye'd like. Are ye too tired to stay?"

"Nay, I can stay longer," but she fooled no one when she rushed to cover her yawn with her hand.

"Right, ye're nae tired at all. Come along. I am taking ye to bed," his wolfish grin promised very little rest, and she could only giggle in return.

"Ma bonnie bride and I are retiring for the evening. It has been an eventful day, and I think we could both do with a rest before tomorrow and the feast."

His farewell was met with resounding cheers from all around. She ducked her head embarrassed that everyone knew exactly why she was tired and how they would most likely be resting.

"Feast?" she whispered as he stepped down from the dais.

"Of course. After the ceremony at the kirk tomorrow, there will be a feast for most of the night."

"There willna be a bedding ceremony now will there?"

"Ye're damn right there willna. Nay mon is seeing ye without a stitch of clothing on," he growled.

"As long as the women understand the same," she growled back but with a yawn escaping, it sounded more like a purr.

Liam kissed her forehead as they made their way into their chamber. He put her down on her feet and turned to lock and bar the door. When he looked back at her, her hair was down, and she ran her fingers through it. He walked over to the table that stood near where the tub previously sat. Hagatha left Kyla's comb, so he picked it up and brought her towards the fire. He sat on the chair and patted his lap.

"Ye dinna need to ask me twice."

When she sat down, he began to run the comb through her hair.

"Mo ionmhas, I havenae ever seen hair that shines like yers. I wish ye wouldnae wear that ugly thing on yer head."

"Ugly? That was yer mother's, and she is the most beautiful woman I have ever seen."

"She may be one of the most beautiful women, but that head cover is horrid. Da canna stand it, and I understand why now."

"I dinna have much choice, and neither does yer mother,

we're married women. She is the lady of the clan, so she canna go around without it."

"But she does. At least, when she is in the family chambers she does. She doesnae wear it when she rides or when we go down to the beach. She kens how much ma da hates it."

Kyla paused for a moment as she considered her options.

"I have only this kertch, so it will have to be washed and returned to yer mother. Until I can make some of ma own, I will wear ma hair up but uncovered. When we are alone here, I willna wear it."

"Ye can wear yer hair pulled back and out of the way, but I will take it down every time I see ye if it is up."

"Giving me orders already, are ye? What if I dinna want to be told how to wear ma hair?"

"I amnae telling ye how to wear it." There was a mischievous glint in his eyes Kyla knew forewarned trouble. "I'm merely warning ye that since I'm taller than ye, I will be able to easily take it down. I maynae want any other mon to see what lies below yer gowns, but I dinna plan to deprive maself entirely either. Ye are beautiful nay matter how ye wear yer hair, but when I see it down, I picture us together."

Kyla twisted to see him, and he groaned as her backside pressed around his already aroused flesh. She reached behind her back and pulled the laces loose. She undid as many as she could reach and then lowered the gown to her shoulders. Liam watched as the material floated down to her waist and pulled the rest loose before she stood up. She let the kirtle drop all the way to the floor before pulling loose the ribbons that held her chemise in place. When that fell to the floor, she walked to the bed and looked back over her shoulder at Liam before she climbed into bed, ensuring he had a clear view of all her backside. Then she laid back and arranged her hair across his pillow.

Liam was already on his feet and pulling his clothes off as quickly as he could. He toed off his boots as he unfastened his brooch and belt. He hung his plaid over the back of the chair and tossed his leine aside before pouncing on her. He leaped onto the bed and dove under the covers. He settled himself between her legs and rested his weight on his elbows. He wrapped tendrils of her hair around his fingers as she ran her hands up and down his back.

"I dinna ken how ma father became so wise, and I dinna ken how I became so lucky, but I do ken I am a fortunate mon. I love ye."

"I love ye, too, Liam. Always and forever."

"Always and forever."

Liam entered her slowly as her body once again became accustomed to their joining. This time, they felt no rush as they explored one another and learned more of what they enjoyed together. It was late into the night when they both were too exhausted to do more than hold each other. Liam held Kyla as she sprawled one arm and leg over him, and he laid one hand over the small of her back. He could not remember ever having been so comfortable before in his life. His final thoughts as he drifted off to sleep were of them standing before the kirk as they exchanged their vows.

CHAPTER NINE

"Lass. Kyla," Liam gently shook his wife awake. *Wife. That sounds better than I could have ever imagined. I like it more every time I say it. After this evening, she will truly be ma wife nae only in my eyes and God's, but in front of everyone's.*

Kyla came awake to the soft sound of Liam's voice near her ear. She blinked her eyes open and looked around. The chamber was still dark, and when she looked past his shoulder, she could not see any rays of sun poking in around the window covers.

"Liam, it isnae even morning yet. I hope this isnae going to be yer routine. I dinna want to be up before the cocks."

Liam pulled her hand down below his waist and grinned.

"Ye arenae up before this cock." He tickled her ribs on the side that did not show any evidence of how the day before started. "And I think ye may come to like that vera routine."

The double entendre was not missed on Kyla as her hand grasped him. She began to stroke him as his fingers slid inside her sheath.

"That wasna why I woke ye, but I dinna mind."

"Hmm. Me neither," she said distractedly as she focused on his fingers rather than his words.

It was not long before both lay panting and smiling. Liam

kissed her quickly before getting out of bed. He pulled a clean leine from his chest and pleated his plaid before wrapping it around his waist. Kyla propped herself up on one elbow as she watched him dress.

I will never grow tired of watching him though I do prefer it when he is getting undressed rather than dressed. He is rather magnificent.

"Ye like what ye see, do ye?"

"Arrogant mon," she laughed as she lobbed a pillow at him.

He easily caught it and tossed it back to her. He moved to a chest that went unnoticed the night before. She crawled to the end of the bed and watched as he lifted the lid to her chest. She realized it was brought to their chamber during the evening meal. Liam pulled out several nightgowns and threw them towards the fire.

"Ye willna be needing those anymore, so they can go in the fire." He rummaged around more as he heard her scamper from the bed. As she tried to run past, his arm shot out and pulled her onto his kneeling lap. "Ye arenae wearing one of those when we are together, and since I dinna plan for us to be apart at night, ye dinna need them."

"Ever so practical, arenae ye?"

"Aye," was all she got in response as he reached around her to pull more clothes from her chest. He settled on a plain and serviceable gown that made him scowl but would serve his purpose. He stood her up and then followed.

"Put this on and grab an extra plaid as an arisaid." When she reached for a chemise, he closed the lid. "Ye dinna need one."

"I canna go aboot half dressed."

"Nay one but me will ken, and ye dinna need it."

She looked at him curiously but got dressed. He had not pressed her for information before then, but now he wanted to ask her about the faded bruises he saw when he examined the ones Randall left. He was determined to learn more before they returned. Once she was ready, they quietly left their chamber and made their way below stairs. They tiptoed past the Great Hall and the various single men who were sleeping there. The Sinclair laird and his wife ensured all single women shared chambers below stairs. The laird was adamant no woman in the Sinclair clan be harassed or compromised while on their land. Only male servants slept in the Great Hall, and single guardsmen slept in the barracks. Married servants lived in their own crofts within the bailey wall.

When they reached the kitchens, they snuck in, and Liam began sorting through the larder. He came back with a wheel of cheese, a loaf of crusty bread from the day before, leftover fowl, and four apples, and he carried a wineskin slung over his shoulder. He looked around and found a small basket near the hearth. He deposited the food and wineskin in there and then took Kyla's hand, leading them through the door that led to the bailey. They walked briskly to the stables where not even the stable boys were stirring yet, and only the first few pink rays of the sun were peeking over the horizon.

Kyla led her horse out of the stall and joined Liam outside the stable. Before she could lift her foot to the stirrup, she felt herself flying as Liam hoisted her in the saddle.

"I ken ye ken ye *can* do it, but ye *dinna have* to do it. Besides, I amnae going to turn down an opportunity to wrap ma hands around ye." Liam grinned almost boyishly. This was the most relaxed Kyla had ever seen him.

They rode towards the gate, and Liam called out quietly for it to be raised. They bent low and made their way to the path that led to the loch. They rode quietly until they got to the loch. Kyla was prepared to stop there, but Liam had other plans.

"Nae there. Just a wee further. To the top of that ridge," he pointed to a cliff not too far in the distance.

Kyla remembered he said the beach was on the other side. She spurred her horse forward first into a canter and then a gallop. She leaned low over her horse's neck and gathered his mane in her hands along with the reins while rising slightly over the seat of her saddle. The wind picked up her hair, and she relished the feeling of flying over the ground with her first real friend. She could barely hear Liam's horse's hooves over the sound of her own horse's hoofbeats. She sensed more than knew where Liam and *Segrr* were. She urged *Vinr* on, and while he might have been a gelding, he was still as competitive as any stallion. As they made their way up the incline, she thought Liam was saying something, but the wind swept away his words. When she was nearly at the crest of the ridge, she reined in *Vinr* and came to a stop. Liam was only feet behind her. He jumped from the saddle and pulled her out of hers before she could cheer her own victory.

"Dinna ever, *ever*, do something so foolhardy and reckless again. I ken we've raced often but on safe ground. Ye could have plunged over that bluidy cliff and been dead before I could get to ye. Dinna *ever* scare me like that again, or I will turn ye over ma knee and paddle yer beautiful backside."

Kyla could feel Liam shaking as he gripped the outside of her shoulders, and he held her eye level with her feet swinging slightly. She lightly placed her hands on his shoulders and smiled down at him.

"Dinna scold me because ye couldnae beat me. Ye told me this was a cliff, so I kenned it ended with a drop, so I reined in. Look, *Vinr* isnae even close to the edge. Ye simply dinna like nae winning. Dinna be a sore loser."

Kyla thought the vein in Liam's neck was going to pop, and she could see the one that ran along his temple pulsating. He pulled her down with him as he sat and laid her over his lap.

"Dinna ye dare! I amnae a wean. Ye canna do this, Liam. I—"

"Ye're nae a wean and should ken better. I dinna want ma wife dead before we even make it to the ceremony! Ye could have broken yer bluidy neck or killed yerself!"

Liam started to pull up her skirts, but the moment he felt Kyla's fight go out of her, and she braced herself, Liam felt like he was going to be ill. He lifted her out of his lap and ran to a nearby bush where he retched. Kyla was left completely dumbfounded and not entirely sure about what happened. Liam was bent over double with his sides heaving. She approached slowly and placed her hand on his back.

"Liam?" she said softly.

When Liam stood up, Kyla was shaken at how pale he was, and she was sure she saw tears in his eyes.

"Kyla, I am so vera sorry. I never should have raised ma hand, or even threatened to raise ma hand, at ye in anger. Ye scared years off ma life, but I will never hit ye. I canna even begin to tell ye how horrid I feel for treating ye so poorly. I willna be that kind of mon to ye. Ye dinna deserve it again."

"Again?"

"I saw the older bruises healing under the ones Randall gave ye. They were old enough that they must have been from when ye were still at yer father's keep."

Kyla nodded her head slowly trying to decide how to respond. She looked at Liam, and her heart broke a little to see her brave and strong warrior husband laid low by his own guilt.

"Liam, aye, ma father did beat me, and while it wasna often, he did do it just before I left. I didna exactly want to come here to marry a mon I didna ken and heard was the size of a caber and aboot as kind. We got into quite the row, and he didna want to hear any more of ma argie bargie, so he ended it with a fine thrashing."

She pressed up on Liam's shoulder, so he would stand up and look at her. She placed her hands over his chest, and he saw her bite her bottom lip before speaking again.

"Liam, ye arenae aught like ma father. He didna pay any attention to me except to let me ken he wished I was a son. He didna treat me differently from ma brothers, really, when I think aboot it. He couldnae thrash me in the lists, so he did it in the keep behind his solar door, but he was as hard on them as he was me. Ye arenae like that. Ye have never made me fear for ma safety, and even when I have seen ye deadly angry, I have never felt like ye would harm me. I didna mean to scare ye like that. I thought a race would be fun, and I remembered ye'd said it was a cliff, so I kenned to slow down before reaching the top. I didna think I was doing aught that risky, but I also didna mean to upset ye. Ye ken, sometimes fear comes out as anger. We dinna ken how to deal with it, and so we lash out. I think mayhap that is exactly what happened here."

Liam looked down at his tiny wife, awestruck at how forgiving and wise she was. He opened his arms, and she stepped into them.

"Ye may be ready to forgive me, but I amnae so quick to forgive maself. I am sorry, mo ghaol."

"I ken," she said as she burrowed into his chest, and he wrapped his arms around her more tightly.

"Actually, I think I ken when I wouldnae mind a little spank now and again." She pulled on his leine and when he bent forward, she cupped her hand around his ear. "Mayhap when ye are behind me. Or even when I'm on top. A little slap might be fun."

She pulled away, leaving him speechless yet again, and began to run towards the slope leading to the beach.

"Catch me if ye can!"

Liam moved faster than he thought he could as he threw the horses' reins over a nearby bush and grabbed their picnic basket before chasing her down to the sand.

They spent the rest of the morning and early afternoon walking along the beach collecting seashells and watching the tide lap against the shore. Once the sun fully rose, it was quite warm, and Kyla shed her arisaid, shoes, and stockings. She dug her toes into the sand and let the grains run between her toes. She looked to the north and saw the end of the headland. The beach narrowed at that point, but to the south, she saw what looked like the entrance to a cave.

"Is that an opening in the rocks over there?"

"Aye, there is an inlet leading to a cave that can be accessed when the tide is low. There is a hidden warm water pool towards the vera back. The light streams in from a hole above but makes it look as though it is illuminated from below. Almost like it glows. But ye must never be there when the tide changes. If ye dinna get out before the tide rises, ye will be trapped in there. Right now, the tide is too high to show ye, but I will sometime soon."

"Did ye play in there when ye were a lad?"

"Did? Dinna ye mean do? I still like to explore in there. I find something new each time even after all these years." Liam gave her a lopsided smile that gave her a rare glimpse at what he must have looked like when he was younger. She felt an overwhelming urge to ruffle his hair.

She looked out over the open water and spotted a pod of young seals playing beyond the surf. The rest of the rookery were sunning themselves on the rocks further north. She pulled the laces from her kirtle and shimmied out of her gown. Liam was caught off guard as she let her kirtle fall to the ground. With no chemise underneath, she was naked in a matter of seconds. She ran to the water's edge and waded in. When the water was waist deep, she dove under the waves and swam out as far as she could before having to come up for air. She rolled to her back and waved to Liam who was disrobing as fast as he could. She flipped back over and swam out further until she was close enough to see the seals' whiskers but could not touch them. While they might have looked sweet and soft, she knew they were still wild animals with parents not far away. She treaded water until Liam joined her.

"Ye arenae angry I swam out this far, are ye?"

"Nay. I'm only shocked ye would want to swim in this freezing water. Ma bullocks are pulled so tight, they may have disappeared inside me."

Kyla laughed loudly enough that several seals barked in response which only made her laugh harder. A few of the pups swam towards them but kept a healthy distance, both human and animal aware and wary.

"The water is always cold in the North Sea, and it wasna any better when I would visit ma friend, Rose MacLeod, and we swam in the Minch. It wasna any better than here. I may be a bit small, but I am sturdy."

She dropped under the water and tugged at his calf as she swam around him. He caught her leg and dragged her back towards him. He grasped her hips and pulled her close. She wrapped her legs around his waist.

"I dinna think ye are feeling the cold overly much after all," she gave him a saucy smile.

Liam rolled to his back and propelled them back towards the coast. His powerful arms and legs made short work of the distance even with the added weight of Kyla clinging to him. The seal pups slapped the water with their fins as though they were saying goodbye. The chorus of barks followed the couple as they came to shallower water, and Liam could stand. Kyla pulled herself around to his back, and he walked from the water with Kyla's arms and legs wrapped around him. When they reached their clothes, she began to disentangle herself, but he stopped her before he spread his plaid out on the sand. He lowered them to the ground and gently laid Kyla on her back.

"Ye dinna weigh more than a feather. I have carried men five and six times yer size around the lists before. But ye do feel a bit chilled after yer dip. Isnae that what ye said ye liked to do? Go for a dip?"

"Aye, and I ken the best way ye can warm me is from the inside out." She let her knees fall wide as he settled between them.

Their hands explored and rubbed the blood back into their arms and legs. It was not long before they both were starting to feel overheated. Liam's fingers slid into Kyla as she wrapped her hand around him. They both started slowly, but as their passion sparked, their patience fizzled. It was not long before they came together, and Liam plunged into Kyla over and over as her hands found the grooves along the side of his hips she loved so much. She rocked her hips to match his thrusts. It did not take long for them both to be left breathless and panting. Liam rolled to his side, and Kyla slid next to him and draped her arm over his ribs. He brushed the hair from her shoulders and stared into the blue eyes he was coming to know better than anything else. He understood the shades of blue they changed between when she was angry, sad, happy, or passionate. He knew cornflower blue was a sure sign that things were well, and she was happy. The lapis lazuli he saw upon meeting her came out when she was angry or frustrated. The deep shade of blue her eyes went when she was sad matched the waters of the North Sea they so recently swam in, and they snapped a sparkling sapphire when filled with passion and pleasure. Liam never imagined he would know the differing hues of a woman's eyes, and he did not know any other woman's eyes, but he would be intrigued for the rest of his life by the ever-changing colors of the windows to his wife's soul.

"I dinna want to leave here, but Hagatha and ye mother will be done in if I dinna return in time to get ready for the ceremony."

Liam nodded as he kissed the corner of her lips and ran his tongue along them.

"Mmm, salty."

"And sandy, I am sure."

They redressed and made their way back to their horses. Liam helped her into the saddle again, and this time she was not taken by surprise when she felt herself soaring upwards. As they started towards the keep, Liam offered the challenge of a race, and Kyla did not disappoint. *Segrr* and *Vinr* were not willing to lose to the other, so horses and riders arrived at the portcullis winded but happy.

Arabella, Hagatha, and Elspeth were awaiting their return on the steps to the keep. They herded Kyla indoors with tsks and harumphs directed over their shoulders at Liam who could do nothing better than grin. He had a wedding to prepare for.

CHAPTER TEN

It was midafternoon when Liam and Kyla returned to the keep after their day spent on the beach, and it was nearly sunset when Kyla was finally led from her old chamber to the Great Hall. She saved the azure blue kirtle she wore now specifically for her wedding day.

After bathing and having the salt and sand scrubbed from her hair by a mildly irritated Hagatha, the women who came to her chamber helped her arrange her hair in braids and curls with ribbons woven through. She wore a matching azure ribbon that sat back from her forehead and kept the few loose strands from breaking through. While she dressed, a parcel arrived for her. She opened it and found a plaid clearly woven for the laird's family. On top of the folded length of fabric was a beautiful Cairngorm brooch. Kyla picked it up and turned it over slowly in her hands as she watched the light catch in the dark topaz center stone.

"Liam's eyes," she said to herself.

"Aye. They do match rather well," Arabella said from behind her. She helped Kyla wrap the plaid over her left shoulder and pin it with the brooch as tradition dictated for the tánaiste's wife. "He sent a messenger the day ye arrived to fetch such a brooch to be yer wedding gift."

"He did?"

"When ye put him in his place so easily, I think he kenned at that moment ye would be his perfect mate. He sent off for it that vera day."

Kyla looked down at her left shoulder as she listened to Arabella. She was deeply moved by the endearing gift and could not wait to let Liam know how much she appreciated his thoughtfulness. She had managed to convince the older women to let her stop in the chamber she now shared with Liam as they had made their way to her old one. She had pulled her own gift for him out of her chest and set it upon the top of his. She had stitched a new saffron colored leine for him which included a larger "L" entwined with a slightly smaller "K" sewn onto each cuff. On the hem, where it would only be seen by Liam unless he went around without a plaid to cover it, she had stitched first a very small pattern of a raven flying over a deerhound, a bear, and a bore, and to the right, she had stitched a larger pattern with an eagle flying beside a red stag and wildcat. She hoped he liked her gift as much as she did his.

When she was finally deemed ready, she followed Arabella down the stairs to the Great Hall where they joined Donnell. They made their way to the steps of the keep and were about to walk to the kirk when they were stopped by a guardsman calling out to Donnell.

"Riders approach, ma laird. Sutherlands."

Kyla looked at Donnell and Arabella but could only shake her head at their questioning look. She turned to look at the kirk and could barely make out the large shape of Liam standing at the doors awaiting her. She turned back to the gate in time to see her brother, Hamish, ride through with her uncle and several of the Sutherland guardsmen behind them. Hamish wore a look that made her want to run far away and fast. A wave of foreboding washed over her as he dismounted and stepped towards her.

"Kyla."

"Hamish. What're ye doing here?"

Hamish did not answer but extended his arm to Donnell who grasped it around the forearm. They shook, and then he kissed Arabella's hand.

"Hamish?"

Her brother turned to her and held out his hand, but Kyla was suddenly blocked by a massive shadow that fell across her. She did not see Liam elbow his way through the crowd to reach her, and she was surprised he was able to move so quickly with most of the clan crowding the bailey.

"Hamish, ye are in time for yer sister's wedding. I hope ye dinna plan to keep us waiting." The warning was evident in Liam's tone if not from the scowl on his face.

"I didna realize today would be the big day. I thought ye would have been wedded weeks ago when Kyla arrived." He leaned over to look around Liam and tried to make eye contact with Kyla, but Liam simply took up too much space. He planted his feet and crossed his arms as he looked down at Hamish, using his spot two steps above his soon-to-be brother by marriage to his advantage. Kyla placed a hand on Liam's arm as she stepped around him. His hands immediately slid around her waist, and he drew her back to his chest. He could not have made his claim more obvious short of carrying her away over his shoulder. Hamish could only nod his head.

"Hamish, something isnae right. Ye look awful. Tell me what's happened because ye're making me uneasy. Why is Uncle Henry here with ye?" She tried not to let her disgust show, but she never liked her uncle and was glad to discover he departed without saying goodbye when he left her with the Sinclairs.

"Can I speak with ye for a moment?" His eyes shifted off to the side indicating he did not want their family business aired out like the morning's laundry.

Kyla looked back at Liam and took one of his hands as she led both men to the garden gate. Liam reached past and unlatched it, allowing Kyla to move towards the Lady's garden. Once the three of them were out of earshot of anyone else, Kyla found herself suddenly assuming the same stance she now associated with Liam. She held her arms crossed, and feet planted widely. Liam struggled not to chuckle when he saw her. For a man his size, the pose was intimidating, but for a woman as petite as his wife, she looked more ornery than imposing. Either way, he was glad she was on his side.

"Hamish, I am supposed to be at the kirk saying ma vows right now. Why are ye here? What has happened? Dinna keep me waiting any longer," she tapped her toe in rhythm to her words.

"They're dead, Kyla. All of them." Hamish choked out the words as he ran a hand through his already disheveled hair.

"Who?"

Kyla looked her brother over and finally began to take in subtle details she initially missed. She noticed the rip in his leine below his raised arm, the dirt around his calves and his neck, the dried blood on his plaid and near his hairline. She stepped forward and brushed the hair back from beside his ear. She turned his chin away as she inspected the dirt-encrusted gash that ran from slightly in front of the bottom of his ear down his neck. It was not deep but jagged.

"Hamish, what's happened? Ye're injured and here with Uncle Henry. Something is vera wrong."

"Father, Dougal, and Murdoch raided the Rosses a fortnight ago, nae long after they returned from gathering back the heads of cattle the Rosses stole from us. I stayed behind to guard the clan. Apparently, they squared off against the Rosses and had the leg up but took for granted that the Rosses would retreat. Instead, Father, Dougal, and Murdoch led them straight to our gates. The Rosses razed three villages along the way and burned out the fields to the west of the keep. We could see the raiding party riding across the meadow from the battlements, but before we could sound any type of warning, the Rosses gained ground and surrounded them. Uncle Henry, two scores of the guardsmen, and I rode out. By the time we got there, Father and our brothers were dead, and I was fighting to keep the Rosses from laying siege to the castle. We were able to beat them back, and they retreated. I havenae seen hide nor hair of them since, but I rode straight here as soon as I kenned the keep was secure."

"Kyla, I'm the new laird," Hamish hung his head and shook it. "I never wanted this. Dougal wanted to be Murdoch's second more than I ever did. I was happy to train the men and ride off to battle. Now, I dinna have a choice but to lead. I refused to take ma oath as the new laird until I told ye. I was hoping ye might be willing to come back to Sutherland while I sort everything out. I dinna have anyone to run the keep, and it's already been falling down around our ears. Ye ken Dougal's and Murdoch's wives arenae any help. They will probably, hopefully, return to their own clans. Now I must be gone while I oversee the repairs to the villages. Kyla, I canna do this alone. I admit that."

Hamish looked from his sister to the man who was supposed to be his brother by marriage and felt the last seeds of hope whither. Kyla felt the solid wall of Liam's chest behind her as she tried to take in all that Hamish told her. In the space of a few minutes, she learned that not only had her entire family been killed but now she may have to return home.

Nay. That isnae home. Home is here with Liam and the rest of the Sinclairs. I dinna ken if I will go back to the Sutherland territory, but if I do, it isnae for forever. I willna stay there, and I willna give up Liam.

As though he read her mind, he turned her towards him and pressed her to him. He rubbed circles on her back as he stroked her hair. She slowly brought her arms around him and breathed in the scent that was uniquely his. She squeezed her eyes shut as if she could block out the rest of the world and focus only on Liam holding her up. He kissed her crown as he brushed away tears she was not even aware were falling.

"We will go to the kirk now, and in the morning, we will set off with ye," Liam said over her head.

She squeezed him more tightly grateful he was making this decision while she felt like she was walking through fog. It felt like an eternity before she was ready to pull back from Liam, and he let her but kept her in the circle of his arms.

"Leannan, are ye ready? We shall go to the kirk and be officially married. Then we can retire directly to our chamber. I'd like ye to try to get some sleep if ye can. It will be a long journey."

"Mo chridhe, I canna do this alone. I dinna want to leave ye."

Kyla looked up at Liam with her tear-filled eyes that matched the North Sea. Her sadness nearly crushed him. He knew what went unspoken. She felt grief for her lost family and clansmen, but she also worried she might not return if she traveled alone.

"Ye are ma wife already. There isnae any year and a day even if we did handfast. We will be wedded by the church, but it is only an affirmation and public announcement of what we already ken. Where ye go, I follow. Ye arenae leaving this keep or this land without me, mo ghaol."

"Thank ye," she choked out. "I love ye."

"And I love ye."

Hamish watched the couple and was relieved to see his sister had finally found the happiness she was deprived while growing up.

"Kyla, a moment more before ye go."

She turned to look at the only brother who ever paid attention to her. She felt guilty that she was relieved he was the one to survive and even more guilty that her grief was for the villagers and crofters who lost everything, not for her family. Her consuming guilt was capped off by her wish to stay with the Sinclairs and not travel back to the Sutherlands. She did not feel like they were her clan anymore. She had not since she arrived here.

"Lass, I ken we were horrible to ye. I was as bad as the others. Mayhap nae in word, but in deed when I didna support ye or protect ye. I lacked the gumption to do what I always kenned was right. It was much easier to stay quiet and let Dougal and Murdoch do as they wanted than make maself their target. I ken Father was as cruel to ye as he was to us in the way he beat ye, but he was especially cruel in constantly reminding ye that he didna have any use for ye. I admit I feared him too much to go against him." He looked up at Liam before he continued, unsure how his confession was being received by both his sister and her husband, a man that was even larger than he was. "I admit I breathed a sigh of relief that I dinna have to live with those three ever again, and I am guilty of nae feeling more grief that they are gone. I am all that is left on that land of the laird's family. I amnae at all prepared to take on these duties, but I willna be aught like Father or Murdoch. I willna lead as they did with intimidation and force. Please, ken ye are always welcome in yer home. I dinna want ye to ever feel unwanted by our clan again, and more importantly, never by me again. I do need yer help, and so I am asking ye to please assist me but only long enough to get ma feet under me. Ye and yer husband will leave whenever ye feel ye must. I dinna want ye to feel trapped again. I'm sorry."

Kyla tapped Liam's arm, and he released her. She stepped forward to Hamish and paused before embracing him.

"I ken. They were nae an easy lot to live with, and I understand yer guilt as I feel the same. But Hamish, that isnae ma home anymore. Ma home and ma clan are with the Sinclairs; however, I will stay with ye for as long as ye need me. Yer apology means a great deal to me and goes far to help smooth things over. I dinna wish for us to be at odds anymore since ye were the one person who did help me get through our childhood. I will help ye in any way I can, but I will nae stay if ye dinna treat me well. Liam and I have responsibilities here too that I willna shirk if I amnae wanted with the Sutherlands."

"That is more than fair."

Kyla wanted to believe her brother, and she was almost sure she could trust him despite the old wounds that still felt so fresh. She would do what she could to help Hamish become the new laird if for no other reason than she wanted the alliance formed by her betrothal with Liam to stand. The Sutherlands and Sinclairs had long held enmity between them, and that was the reason for her marriage. She did not want to add to the Sutherlands' current burden or Hamish's.

"What of the Rosses," Liam finally spoke up.

"I dinna ken, to be honest. We havenae seen or heard from them. I ken they suffered several losses too, but I dinna think they will be licking their wounds for long. I expect them to retaliate again."

"If ye can house and feed them, I will bring three score men with us."

Hamish's eyes became as wide as saucers at this announcement.

"I willna risk ma wife's safety on the road or at yer keep. We pledged to become allies with ma marriage to Kyla. This is how we shall support ye. But hear me now just as well as ye did Kyla. If ye in anyway mistreat her, we will leave that vera day, whether the sun shines or nae. If anyone speaks ill of her or to her, I will pull ma men and the alliance ends."

Liam extended his hand to Hamish who paused for only a second before grasping Liam's forearm. They shook, and the agreement was sealed.

"Lass, we've kept ye waiting long enough. Ye have a wedding to attend, and I have a wife to marry. Again." He smiled down to her as they took each other's hand and walked to the kirk.

CHAPTER ELEVEN

The entire clan gathered to witness the marriage of Liam Sinclair and Kyla Sutherland. It was an auspicious occasion after the ongoing strife between the Sutherlands and Sinclairs, and many of the clan members witnessed the budding romance between the laird's son and his betrothed. The events of the previous day were forgotten for the moment, and the excitement in the air was nearly palpable as Liam and Kyla stood before the priest on the steps of the kirk to recite their vows before the crowd. Standing facing one another, Father Michael wrapped a swath of Sinclair plaid around their wrists, binding them as their words soon would.

"I, Liam Donnell Magnus Sinclair, in the name of the spirit of God that resides within us all, by the life that courses within ma blood and the love that resides within ma heart, take thee, Kyla Isabella Anne Sutherland, to ma hand, ma heart, and ma spirit, to be ma chosen one. To desire thee and be desired by thee, to possess thee, and be possessed by thee, without sin or shame, for naught can exist in the purity of ma love for thee. I promise to love thee wholly and completely without restraint, in sickness and in health, in plenty and in poverty, in life and beyond, where we shall meet, remember, and love again. I shall nae seek to change thee in any way. I shall respect thee, thy beliefs, thy people, and thy ways as I respect maself."

"I, Kyla Isabella Anne Sutherland, take ye, Liam Donnell Magnus Sinclair, to be ma partner in life and ma one true love. I will cherish our friendship, and I will love ye today, I will love ye tomorrow, and I will love ye forever. I will trust ye, and I will honor ye. I will laugh with ye, and I will cry with ye. I will love ye faithfully through the best and the worst. I will love ye through the difficult and the easy. What may come, I will always be there as today I have given ye ma hand to hold, so do I give ye ma life and ma heart to forever keep."

"It's done. Ye are ma wife in all ways now. I willna be without ye ever again. I love ye till ma last breath, ye and only ever ye," Liam spoke softly enough for only Kyla to hear.

"Ye are ma husband, and I couldnae ask for more. I am blessed with the life we shall build here. I love ye, and ma love will only grow with the years as it is for ye and only ever ye," Kyla responded as Liam looked into her cornflower blue eyes that dazzled him from the very beginning.

I wonder if any of our bairns will have her eyes. I dinna think I would ever be able to say nay if they do. Heaven help me if it is a lass born looking like her mother.

Liam led Kyla, their hands still bound together, into the kirk for the wedding mass. Only the family followed the couple where the mass proceeded, and the final blessing was given. When Liam and Kyla's kiss at the end of the mass seemed to carry on for longer than was proper, there were several throats cleared and a few discreet coughs, but neither of them was in a hurry to end the moment. When they finally drew apart, Liam slid their hands free of the plaid and scooped Kyla up before carrying her to the Great Hall. Kyla ran her fingers through and played with the hair that lay below the collar of Liam's leine. She brushed a thick lock from over his eyes while smiling up at him.

I hope our sons are like him, braw and protective of all who rely upon them, and I hope our daughters are as kind and wise as their da.

Liam arrived at their places at the dais, and the evening meal soon began. The newlywed couple stayed through all the courses but only a few of the toasts. As Liam once again carried Kyla to their chamber, the merriment of the wedding feast carried on without them. Their handfast was known to all, so no bedding ceremony would happen for which Kyla was extremely grateful.

"Ye ken, I wouldnae ever have allowed a bedding ceremony even if we hadnae handfasted," Liam murmured in her ear and laughed at her surprise. "I kenned that was what ye were thinking about."

"And I ken that I can walk just as well as anyone else with two legs. People will begin to think me infirm if ye carry me everywhere."

"Nay. The women will think me romantic, and the men will think me lucky."

They arrived at their chamber door which Kyla leaned over to open, and Liam kicked it shut once they crossed the threshold. They slowly undressed one another before climbing into bed. Their union had already been consummated, more than once, but they took their time making love, reveling in the knowledge there was nothing that could now separate them. They fell asleep, only to awake what felt like moments later and prepared for their long journey.

The next fortnight was long and difficult. The terrain was rough, and it rained off and on most days. There were only a handful of nights that Liam was able to arrange for them to stay at an inn, so the rest was spent out under the moon and stars. Even though they fooled no one, as newlyweds, they craved more time alone, so they fully used the fact that Kyla was the only woman in the traveling party to give them the opportunity to sneak off alone.

They were slowed further when one of the horses threw a

shoe and another went lame. The entire group was weary, travel-stained, and famished when they arrived. Kyla hoped it would a good long while before she ate another bannock or strip of dried beef. Liam was ready for a hearty meal and a soft bed. They finally rode into the Sutherland keep, Forse Castle, as the sun began to set on the fifteenth day of travel.

"Ma laird, we are happy ye have returned with Lady Kyla," an older woman approached the group smiling warmly.

"Flora!" Kyla rushed forward and was nearly swallowed by the bosom of the woman who was clearly the chatelaine. The massive ring of keys jingled from her waist as she warmly hugged Kyla. "Ye're the housekeeper now?"

"Aye, lass. It was the one thing Hamish declared before leaving. Molly has a croft of her own, and we all breathe easier. It is good to have ye home. I wasna sure ye would come back to us, but I am mighty pleased ye did."

Kyla pulled away and looked over her shoulder to find Liam. He hung back to give her a moment with a woman who was clearly very fond of his wife. Kyla reached out her hand and gestured for him to come forward. She kept holding it out until he took it, then she turned back to Flora.

"Flora, this is ma husband, Liam Sinclair. We have come only long enough to help Hamish get settled into the lairdship. Ye ken Liam is the tánaiste for Clan Sinclair, so we canna be away for too long. Flora, ma home isnae here anymore. Ma home is with the Sinclairs, with Liam."

Flora looked Kyla over from head to toe and smiled brightly even if there were tears in her eyes.

"Ye had a rough start to yer life since yer mother passed, but I can see ye are where ye were always meant to be. Married life seems to suit ye." She took in the sight of the imposing warrior who hovered nearby. "Lad, ye dinna need to fash. Yer lady didna have an easy go of it here, and I dinna want to speak ill of the dead, but it was her father's and brothers' doing. Nay one else in the clan agreed with how they treated her, but who was to speak against the laird?"

Liam nodded his head slowly. He knew the woman spoke the truth, but that did not ease his anger when he remembered the old bruises he found nor when he remembered what Kyla told him about her life with her family.

"Och, ye dinna believe me, do ye?"

"I do, but I am still wary that nay one mistreats ma wife again."

Flora looked at Kyla and winked.

"He does seem to like calling ye that. I think he's quite chuffed to have ye by his side," she said in a stage whisper.

"I ken he is, but I'll admit he's more than just fair to middling."

"Perhaps we could move this inside, and Kyla could be given something to eat and a bath arranged," Liam suggested none too subtly.

"Right ye are. Come, lassie. I'll make sure yer chamber is ready." Flora looked at Liam once more, "then again, mayhap we shall put ye in a guest chamber. I dinna think yer bed will hold this mon. He'll come crashing through the floorboards."

Kyla laughed before wrapping her arm around Liam's waist.

"Ma bed was rather small by most standards, but it was fine for me. Ye wouldnae even fit half of ye on it, ma braw mon."

Liam leaned over and kissed her temple before whispering in her ear.

"We dinna need a bed for what I'm thinking aboot." He laughed when Kyla's face went beet red. "Dinna act like ye were nae thinking aboot the same thing that last stretch while ye rode in front of me."

"Sshh. I may have been, but ye dinna need to say it aloud."

"For yer ears, and eyes, only." He tapped her gently on the backside as they made their way into the keep.

A moon passed before Liam and Kyla were ready to return to Sinclair land. In the time they spent with the Sutherlands, Kyla came to understand the extent of her father's highhandedness when more of the clan members greeted her warmly and accepted her among them. No one outwardly shunned her other than her family, but others felt nervous to show her favor in case the laird became aware. Now that Hamish was installed as the new laird, the entire atmosphere within Forse Castle was lighter, and there was laughter that did not come at someone else's, primarily Kyla's, expense.

Liam and Hamish worked with the Sutherland guardsmen every day, going out to the lists well before the sun rose and coming back moments before the evening meal. On the days when they did not spend its entirety in the lists, they visited the local crofters and farmers to ensure they had all they needed and were prepared in case of another raid. Kyla worked with the women to plan and begin preparing for the winter months. The weather was already starting to turn cold, and the clan needed to have plenty of food dried and stored well before the first snow. Kyla also made visits to the village to inspect the crofters' homes for any repairs needed to be made or for supplies that might be running short.

Every evening, Kyla and Liam met in their chamber. Some nights they returned to the Great Hall for the last meal of the day, but more often than not, they took a tray in their chamber. They craved the time alone with one another, and even though they were both exhausted, they spent time both talking and making love. It became a routine they enjoyed. They would share different snippets and anecdotes from their day while bathing, they would make plans for the next day over their meal, and then fall into bed and make love before falling asleep in one another's arms. By the end of their stay, Kyla felt assured that Hamish was not only going to be a strong laird but that the entire clan was already better off for the change. She finally felt welcome even though she was ready to go home with Liam.

They set off early one morning with their three score guardsmen. The weather was on their side this time, and they made fair progress each day. While the weather was pleasant, and the ride was made easier with no unforeseen problems with the horses, Kyla struggled to stay awake by midafternoon and often could not muster the appetite to choke down the dried beef and bannocks. Liam insisted she ride with him from when they stopped to rest the horses at midday until they stopped for the night. He was becoming increasingly agitated when Kyla did not seem to regain any of her usual vibrancy and energy after nearly a sennight of travel. He began whittling about how little she ate, whether she was getting enough sleep and whether they should stop to rest more often. Kyla finally came to the end of her patience one afternoon when they stopped to water the horses, and she needed to find yet another bush.

"I hope ye arenae going to be like this for the next nine moons. I dinna think ye or I will make it. I may be having a bairn, but I amnae a bairn. Dinna fash like a mother hen. I—"

"Bairn?" Liam choked

"Och, bluidy hell! That wasna at all how I planned to tell ye. But aye, a bairn. I hope ye dinna hover like this when the lad or lass is born. Ye canna be carrying on like this." She waved a hand around in her agitation.

"I dinna care. I'm going to be a da!"

Liam plucked his bonnie little wife off the ground and twirled her around as she laughed over and over.

EPILOGUE

Kyla, mo leannan, I dinna ken how I've made it this long without ye. Every day has been a trial since ye left us. If it were nae for our children, and now their bairns, I dinna think I would have survived without ye. There isnae a day that goes by that I dinna think of ye. I canna walk into our chamber without remembering how ye looked before ye fell asleep or when ye first opened yer eyes.

The good Lord took ye from us far too soon. If only ye could have seen how well our lads and our lassie turned out. Ye would be proud, just as I was always proud to call ye mine. There hasnae been anyone else since the day I laid eyes on ye, and ye told me I sounded like a stung bear or was it a stuck bore. Mo aon ghaol mòr, my one great love. I pledged that to yer twice. Do ye remember? 'Through all our lives together, in all our lives, may we be reborn that we may meet and ken and love again and remember.' I dinna think our children are quite ready for me to leave them, but I long for the day when we might be joined together again. Och, but it is so vera hard. I told ye true, mo chridhe. Ye are ma love 'in life and beyond, where we shall meet, remember, and love again.' I ken ye watch over us, and I thank God for it always, but it still pains me ye arenae here with me. Do ye see what joy ye have given me? What blessings we shared. Kyla, thank ye, lass. I love ye.

"Da, did ye hear aught that I said?" Tavish sounded aggrieved.

"Nay, I didna. What was that again?"

"Dinna tell us ye're getting to be a mincey heid bodach."

"Da is neither addlepated nor an auld mon. Be nice, Tavish, or I'll make ye change Wee Liam's raggies again." Mairghread scolded. "Da, dinna listen to him. He's nae used to nae getting his way. These days, he's having to learn other people's opinions matter as much if nae more than his. He's fussier than a bairn cutting teeth or a bear that got stung for putting his paw in the honeypot."

Liam stared at Mairghread for a moment and then nearly burst with laughter. He laughed so hard that tears began to stream down his cheeks. He used the back of his hand to wipe them again. He looked up to the rafters as he tried to catch his breath.

"Did ye hear that, Kyla?"

"And ye dinna think him a bit of a bampot when he's talking to thin air?"

"He's talking to Mama. Let him be," Callum tutted.

"Yer mama said nearly the same thing to me aboot being a raging bear on the day we met. It reminded me of how poor of an impression I made on her and how dumbstruck I was with her beauty the first time I laid eyes on her. She's still the most beautiful woman I have ever seen." He looked at Mairghread and smiled softly, "I am so fortunate ye look more and more like yer mama every day. Ye have her eyes and her spirit. It lets me ken she is still with us."

"Have ye, ladies, heard the story of how our parents met?" Mairghread asked as she looked to the newer members of the Sinclair clan and the laird's family.

"I havenae."

"Me neither."

"Nay."

"I'd like to."

"Och, well it's quite the tale to be told," Magnus spoke up. "We havenae heard it in quite some time. Da, will ye tell us?"

Liam looked around at the faces of his children and their

families and was reminded of when they used to gather around his own father's lap to hear tales from long ago. He could not help but smile at the eager looks on everyone's face. He reached out, and Mairghread handed Wee Liam, his namesake, to him. Once the toddler settled on his lap, he closed his eyes for a moment.

"I wasna prepared for the surprise of ma life the day I met yer mother. I was in the middle of arguing with ma father aboot getting married when a soft voice came from behind. I kenned right then and there that I was snookered, but I vera nearly swallowed ma own tongue when I turned around and saw yer mother standing there. She didna say all that much, but what she said put me right back in ma place. I still remember it all so clearly."

The rest of the evening was spent around the fire as Laird Liam Sinclair recounted the story of how he fell in love with Lady Kyla Sutherland, or rather Lady Kyla Sinclair. He remembered and retold all that happened during *their Highland beginning.*

THANK YOU FOR READING THEIR HIGHLAND BEGINNING

Celeste Barclay, a nom de plume, lives near the Southern California coast with her husband and sons. Growing up in the Midwest, Celeste enjoyed spending as much time in and on the water as she could. Now she lives near the beach. She's an avid swimmer, a hopeful future surfer, and a former rower. When she's not writing, she's working or being a mom.

Visit Celeste's website, www.celestebarclay.com, for regular updates on works in progress, new releases, and her blog where she features posts about her experiences as an author and recommendations of her favorite reads.

Are you an author who would like to guest blog or be featured in her recommendations? Visit her website for an opportunity to share your insights and experiences.

Have you read *Their Highland Beginning, The Clan Sinclair*

Prequel? Learn how the saga begins! This FREE novella is available to all new subscribers to Celeste's monthly newsletter. Subscribe on her website.

www.celestebarclay.com

Join the fun and get exclusive insider giveaways, sneak peeks, and new release announcements in

Celeste Barclay's Facebook Ladies of Yore Group

THE HIGHLAND LADIES

A Spinster at the Highland Court **BOOK 1 SNEAK PEEK**

Elizabeth Fraser looked around the royal chapel within Stirling Castle. The ornate candlestick holders on the altar glistened and reflected the light from the ones in the wall sconces as the priest intoned the holy prayers of the Advent season. Elizabeth kept her head bowed as though in prayer, but her green eyes swept the congregation. She watched the other ladies-in-waiting, many of whom were doing the same thing. She caught the eye of Allyson Elliott. Elizabeth raised one eyebrow as Allyson's lips twitched. Both women had been there enough times to accept they'd be kneeling for at least the next hour as the Latin service carried on. Elizabeth understood the Mass thanks to her cousin Deirdre Fraser, or rather now Deirdre Sinclair. Elizabeth's mind flashed to the recent struggle her cousin faced as she reunited with her husband Magnus after a seven-year separation. Her aunt and uncle's choice to keep Deirdre hidden from her husband simply because they didn't think the Sinclairs were an advantageous enough match, and the resulting scandal, still humiliated the other Fraser clan members at court. She admired Deirdre's husband Magnus's pledge to remain faithful despite not knowing if he'd ever see Deirdre again.

Elizabeth suddenly snapped her attention; while everyone else intoned the twelfth—or was it thirteenth—amen of the Mass, the hairs on the back of her neck stood up. She had the strongest feeling that someone was watching her. Her eyes scanned to her right, where her parents sat further down the pew. Her mother and father had their heads bowed and eyes closed. While she was convinced her mother was in devout prayer, she wondered if her father had fallen asleep during the Mass. Again. With nothing seeming out of the ordinary and no one visibly paying attention to her, her eyes swung to the left. She took in the king and queen as they kneeled together at their prie-dieu. The queen's lips moved as she recited the liturgy in silence. The king was as still as a statue. Years of leading warriors showed, both in his stature and his ability to control his body into absolute stillness. Elizabeth peered past the royal couple and found herself looking into the astute hazel eyes of Edward Bruce, Lord of Badenoch and Lochaber. His gaze gave her the sense that he peered into her thoughts, as though he were assessing her. She tried to keep her face neutral as heat surged up her neck. She prayed her face didn't redden as much as her neck must have, but at a twenty-one, she still hadn't mastered how to control her blushing. Her nape burned like it was on fire. She canted her head slightly before looking up at the crucifix hanging over the altar. She closed her eyes and tried to invoke the image of the Lord that usually centered her when her mind wandered during Mass.

A Spy at the Highland Court **BOOK 1.5 SNEAK PEEK**
A Companion to the Series

Dedric Hage watched as the English king continued his royal rage as courtiers and advisors eased away from their irate sovereign. His Majesty's face was mottled with red splotches that only accentuated his fair complexion, and spittle formed at the corners of his mouth as his rant amplified. King Edward stalked about the chamber on the long legs that earned him the moniker "Longshanks."

"I don't give a bloody damn who oversaw the attack. It failed!" He railed against the last advisor who tried to reassure him that the recent loss was not the end of his campaign against the Scots. "Failure is failure. That usurper believes he's gotten the upper hand, and he will continue worming his way further into England now that he thinks he has outsmarted me. I should have killed him when I had the chance."

King Edward muttered his final comments as he sank back into the engraved and carved chair that sat on a dais. His bile spewed the king retreated into his own thoughts as the rest of the chamber was left wondering what to do next.

Dedric had seen this pattern countless times over the course of his life. He was all too familiar with the king's mercurial temper and unpredictable outbursts, but he also knew Edward was one of the best strategists and logisticians to have every lived. While he might not like the man, he respected him. At times. Ric watched as the king scanned the crowd, assessing each knight present until his eyes settled on rich, who wished he could melt into the curtains and watch the people in the gardens below.

"Sir Dedric, approach."

A Wallflower at the Highland Court **BOOK 2 SNEAK PEEK**

The din of music and loud conversation–along with the pervasive odor of too many unwashed or over-perfumed bodies crowded into Stirling Castle's Great Hall–gave Maude Sutherland a pounding headache. As she observed the dancers from her position at the side of the chamber, part of her envied the other ladies-in-waiting who twirled with ease and confidence, but mostly she wished for nothing more than the blessed silence of her chamber. While Maude propped up the wall, she spied her younger sister, Blair, who moved through the country reel with what must have been her seventh partner that evening. Though she was only an observer, sweat trickled down Maude's back and between her breasts. A warm snap —unseasonable for spring in the Highlands— had the doors to the terraces wide open. This should have been enough to ease Maude's discomfort, but the breeze did little to offset how her thick brown hair trapped the heat on her head and neck. Unlike most maidens, Maude wore her hair up almost every waking moment. She possessed a massive amount of thick, coarse, mousey brown hair that was unruly even on the best of days. By evening the weight of the hair, regardless of whether it was up or down, pulled on her neck and contributed to her headache. She would have loved nothing more than to cut it all off and wear it short like her father, Laird Hamish Sutherland, or her brother, Lachlan. She envied them the freedom to wear their hair however they wanted.

A crimson gown floated in Maude's periphery, so she turned to watch her closest friend, Arabella Johnstone. She and Arabella were as different as chalk and cheese but had somehow struck up a close friendship. Where Arabella's hair glowed in the candlelight, Maude accepted her hair was dull. Where Arabella's face looked like an artist's masterpiece, Maude was aware she was plain. Where Arabella was petite and lean through her hips and legs, Maude considered herself far too broad across the beam. As she grew into womanhood, her frame filled out, and while she had a bust most women would envy, her hips and legs were proportionate. Whenever Arabella or Blair glided across the dance floor, she recalled the many adjectives her brother and his friends had come up with for her when they were younger. "Sodgy," "bamsey," "bowzy," "jostly," "podg," and "flobbed up" were the ones that always came to mind. Her brother had since repented for the unkind and merciless teasing. Lachlan noticed that the more he and his friends teased Maude, the less she ate. On the day she collapsed and nearly fell down the stairs leading to the family chambers, he was the one to catch her and carry her to her chamber. In her hazy state, she confessed to have only eaten dried fruit and bannocks the previous three days in hopes of slimming. Lachlan never said an unkind word to his sister again and thereafter became fiercely protective of her, fighting more than one friend when they failed to cease teasing her.

A Rogue at the Highland Court **BOOK 3 SNEAK PEEK**

The crunch of frost echoed in Stirling Castle's royal gardens as Allyson Elliot trudged along with the other ladies-in-waiting, enduring another one of the queen's morning strolls through the struggling blossoms. It was mid-March, and spring had arrived for their neighbors to the south, but Mother Nature seemed to have forgotten that Stirling wasn't truly in the Highlands. Sitting on the border between the Highlands and Lowlands, the weather in Stirling was fickle, playing both sides of the fence. Allyson puffed out a cloud of condensation as the ice crackled beneath her booted feet. She didn't mind the distance of the morning constitutional, but having been raised in the Lowlands, Allyson was still unaccustomed to the frigid temperatures of the north.

"I still can't believe he married her." Allyson caught the waspish voice of Cairstine Grant as her attention returned to the young women around her. Allyson realized Cairstine spoke of Maude Sutherland without hearing the former lady-in-waiting's name. Maude had been a shy lass from the northern Highlands, and several of the other ladies-in-waiting—Cairstine Grant included—had teased her without mercy. It had come as a shock when Kieran MacLeod arrived at court and immediately took an interest in Maude, who the other ladies considered overweight and plain. He'd been one of the most eligible lairds, and more than one nose was out of joint when he chose a woman so many believed was beneath him.

Allyson struggled to smother her giggle as she considered just how Maude was beneath Kieran these days. Allyson arrived at court four years ago as an impressionable girl overwhelmed by the attention her fair hair and robin-egg blue eyes garnered. She soon realized she enjoyed the attention after being the youngest of her parents' six children. A few batted eyelashes and a coy smile earned her the appreciation of the young courtiers who flocked to court hoping to gain attention and favor from King Robert the Bruce. While Allyson wasn't as daring as some of her peers, she had stolen a few kisses from these men, hoping to find one who would make her his wife and take her away from both the royal court and her family. Her attempts hadn't garnered a husband, but it had resulted in a reputation as a flirt.

"Allyson. Allyson, are you listening to me?"

A Rake at the Highland Court **BOOK 4 SNEAK PEEK**

Eoin Gordon raised his chalice once more to toast his twin brother, Ewan, and his new sister-by-marriage, Allyson. As he did, he had a sense that someone was watching him. As the hairs on the back of his neck rose, Eoin passed a quick glance over the diners seated below the dais, but no one seemed to be paying attention to him. He raised his chalice again but didn't take a sip; instead, he continued to scan the crowd. He looked for anyone doing the same: studying him while attempting to ensure no one else noticed.

"What's amiss?" Ewan, the elder twin by five minutes and the heir to Clan Gordon, leaned toward him. The brothers had been inseparable since the day of their birth. They possessed an uncanny intuition for one another and seemed to share the same thoughts more often than not. Until Ewan fell in love with Allyson, neither trusted anyone more than they did each other. As he heard Allyson laugh, Eoin's memory flashed to her courtship with Ewan. Their relationship started poorly when Allyson ran away rather than consider a marriage to Ewan. More than once during that time, Eoin had wanted to shake Ewan, whose views on marriage and fidelity had changed all too slowly. Eoin was grateful for Allyson's influence; he was certain his brother was a better man for it.

"Naught. I just have a sense that someone is watching me," Eoin explained. "It's making me want to squirm."

"I haven't a clue why women find you so attractive, but it's probably some bored wife or lonely widow," Ewan grinned. His reputation as a rogue was entrenched in many women's minds, but his obvious devotion to Allyson no longer caused Eoin concern that his brother intended to stray from his marriage vows. "You do have a reputation as a rake. One of them is hoping they'll warm your bed tonight."

"Only one?" Eoin cocked an eyebrow and grinned. "My charm must be slipping."

"You assume you had any to begin with. Perhaps it was my charm that lured the women, and they figured two is better than one," Ewan teased. The twins were mirror images in every way except for their battle scars. Ewan had a scar that split the left corner of his lip, and Eoin had a less noticeable scar above his left eyebrow. While their scares weren't in the same place, they were still on the same side. There was little to distinguish them apart, and they'd relied upon that throughout their lives, often trading places.

"That very charm had me running for the hills," Allyson elbowed her husband as she leaned around Ewan to speak to her brother-by-marriage. "It's Cairstine Grant. I don't have a clue why she keeps looking at you, but she can't seem to distract herself."

"Cairstine? Why would she be staring?" Eoin wondered aloud.

An Enemy at the Highland Court **BOOK 5 SNEAK PEEK**

A crack of thunder followed only moments later by a blaze of lightning made several ladies-in-waiting jump within the queen's solar. The early autumn storm seemed to rattle one's bones as much as it did the window embrasures. Cairren Kennedy glanced around Queen Elizabeth's private salon and stifled her chuckle as the newest ladies-in-waiting trembled. Mostly Lowlanders, these young ladies were not yet accustomed to the raging storms the Highlands flung upon Stirling from the north. Cairren arrived at Robert the Bruce's court three years earlier as a wide-eyed and quiet girl. But in the time she'd spent there, she'd developed a thick skin and a significant cynicism. As she watched the newer arrivals, she wished she could return to her days before becoming a lady-in-waiting to Elizabeth de Burgh. It had been just over a year since her best friend, Allyson Elliot, married Ewan Gordon and moved to the Highlands. During that year, Cairren awaited the announcement of her own betrothal, and with each passing month, she found her mood increasingly matched the weather outside.

Cairren received a hint from her father around the time of Allyson's wedding that he was in the midst of arranging a betrothal to a Highlander, but he'd volunteered no specifics. Cairren suspected that news came several prospective suitors ago. Growing up near the border, with constant strife between the Scots and the English, made life among the contentious Highlanders seem peaceful. While her clan's land sat along the coast, their allies were the Dunbars and Armstrongs, which meant the two border clans often called upon the Kennedys to lend warriors to the cause. She understood her father wanted her away from the ever-shifting political dynamics that were a daily part of life in the south. However, moving to the Highlands sight unseen terrified her. She was blessed with a doting father who always had her best interests at heart, but she couldn't help but wonder how he thought the Highlands were a better option. She'd rather move to her mother's people in southern France. At least there, she would blend in.

"Lady Cairren," Queen Elizabeth's voice drew Cairren out of her pensiveness, forcing her to abandon her thoughts. "Please pick up where you left off yesterday."

Cairren retrieved the vellum copy of *Summa contra Gentiles* from the table upon which she'd laid it the day before. With a slight French lilt to her voice, Cairren was among the queen's favorites to read aloud. She was also one of the few women who read fluently. She accepted that the queen had committed her to an hour of droning prose on providence and the soul. While she was as devout as the next person, Cairren swallowed her sigh as she prepared to read the divine insights of Thomas Aquinas. As she settled onto a stool, a page entered the solar and whispered to the Mistress of the Bedchamber who, in turn, cast an eye at Cairren.

"Your Majesty, I beg your pardon, but Lady Cairren has been summoned to see her father and mother, who are newly arrived," the Mistress of the Bedchamber announced, all eyes swinging to Cairren.

A Saint at the Highland Court BOOK 6 SNEAK PEEK

"Sister," Lachlan Sutherland approached Blair with Arabella Johnstone on his arm. Arabella had been Maude's only other close friend while she was at court. The women had been roommates, and Arabella took Maude—and by extension Blair—under her wing when she arrived. "Every mon in this gathering hall keeps looking at you, and yet you seem to be in a world of your own, uninterested in them. Well done. I approve."

Lachlan grinned at his youngest sibling as Arabella released his arm. He swiped three mugs of ale from a passing servant, handing one to each lady. The three Sutherland siblings were very close, and Blair was ecstatic any time Lachlan appeared at court. The only family she knew that shared this kind of closeness were the Sutherlands' cousins, the Sinclairs. Lachlan wrapped his arm around Blair's shoulders and dropped a kiss on the crown of her head. They hadn't seen one another since Lachlan's unexpected arrival in late autumn, when he accompanied Cairren and Padraig to Stirling, but he had returned to settle the annual taxes their clan owed the crown. The brother and sister enjoyed a fortnight of each other's company. With Maude no longer beside her, Blair was starved for time with her family. Lachlan never shied away from showing his affection for his sisters, and Blair welcomed it.

"Shall I take you for a lap around the floor?" Lachlan inquired as he grinned at Blair. "Or will you prop up this wall a little longer? I may be your brother, but I shall be the envy of every mon with a heartbeat."

A Beauty at the Highland Court **BOOK 7 SNEAK PEEK**

"I just need a few moments more," Blair looked over her shoulder at Arabella.

"You needn't rush. We still have time," Arabella reassured as she dabbed rose water behind her ears and into her cleavage. She knew the Great Hall would be sweltering, and the fresh scent was as much for her as it was for anyone else. It would offer her a reprieve from the stench of too many unwashed and overheated bodies.

As Arabella watched Blair, she wondered when her friend would find her match. She suspected that it would happen soon, since Blair and Hardwin Cameron were inseparable. It wouldn't surprise Arabella if Blair and Hardi (as she called him) handfasted before a priest could read the banns. Thoughts of Maude and Blair inevitably turned her mind toward their older brother, Lachlan. Arabella stifled her sigh as she thought about the handsome, dark-haired man who appeared at court every few months. She didn't envy him his lengthy rides south from Dunrobin. The keep was along the northeastern coast of Scotland, almost as far north as that of the Sinclairs, and marriage linked the two clans. Arabella had long admired Lachlan's easygoing nature and protectiveness of his sisters. The three siblings were extremely close, and both Maude and Blair had looked forward to his visits. Arabella knew Lachlan looked for excuses to see them. She couldn't help the sadness she felt when she realized Lachlan would rarely make the long trip to court once Blair left.

"I'm almost done," Blair said as she bent to pull up her stockings and slip on her shoes. She disliked wearing stockings, so she put them on last.

Arabella thought about her other friends who had left over the past three years. Nearly all her original friends were gone, one after another marrying and leaving court.

THE CLAN SINCLAIR

His Highland Lass **BOOK 1 SNEAK PEEK**

She entered the great hall like a strong spring storm in the northern most Highlands. Tristan Mackay felt like he had been blown hither and yon. As the storm settled, she left him with the sweet scents of heather and lavender wafting towards him as she approached. She was not a classic beauty, tall and willowy like the women at court. Her face and form were not what legends were made of. But she held a unique appeal unlike any he had seen before. He could not take his eyes off of her long chestnut hair that had strands of fire and burnt copper running through them. Unlike the waves or curls he was used to, her hair was unusually straight and fine. It looked like a waterfall cascading down her back. While she was not tall, neither was she short. She had a figure that was meant for a man to grasp and hold onto, whether from the front or from behind. She had an aura of confidence and charm, but not arrogance or conceit like many good looking women he had met. She did not seem to know her own appeal. He could tell that she was many things, but one thing she was not was his.

His Bonnie Highland Temptation **BOOK 2 SNEAK PEEK**

The pounding in Callum's head as he awoke made him wonder if he had been mistaken for the blacksmith's anvil. Slowly, he opened his eyes and looked over at the curvaceous blonde sleeping next to him. The previous night began to drift through his memory. His father, Liam Sinclair the chief of Clan Sinclair, had announced less than a sennight night ago that not only had he arranged a betrothal for Callum, his heir and tánaiste, but that the woman would be arriving before the sennight was over. She was expected some time late this day, so last night he had celebrated his upcoming nuptials by drowning his sorrows in more drams of whisky than he could remember and taking his current lover to bed for a night of entertainment and pleasure. He had been very sure to tell Elizabeth that this was his last night of freedom and that their short, albeit passionate, liaison was coming to an end. While Callum Sinclair may have enjoyed more than a few women's attention and considered himself a well experienced lover, he was also a man committed to fidelity to his wife. Whomever she might be.

His Highland Prize **BOOK 3 SNEAK PEEK**

I just need to make it to the light. Heavenly Father, please let there be a light over this hill. I canna go much farther. I must go farther. Will there never be a village or a keep nearby? I dinna think I will last much longer. Please, in the name of the Father and all the heavenly saints, just let me find someone who can help me.

Brighde Kerr pushed her sopping wet hair from her eyes as she stumbled onward. She had lost her shoes days ago after they had fallen apart while on the run from her pursuers. Her kirtle, which had once been a daffodil yellow was now a murky shade of beige with a ripped sleeve, frayed hem, and at least two holes that she had noticed in the skirts. Brighde ached all over. Her feet were raw from walking and running for nearly two weeks. Her legs protested taking even one more step, and her chest burned from trying to breathe through her efforts and the torrential downpour in which she once again found herself.

Light! I'm sure of it. I can finally see it coming from a keep. Dear God above, please allow me in. I just need---

His Highland Pledge **BOOK 4 SNEAK PEEK**

Magnus Sinclair detested being at the royal court. There was nothing redeemable in his eyes, and his face ensured everyone knew the Highland giant was not there to exchange pleasantries. Standing at six and a half feet tall, he towered over almost every man in the king's household and all the men who sought the monarch's attention. Only a few visiting Highlanders mirrored him in height and physique. As though sticking out like a sore thumb from his height and his insistence upon wearing his plaid was not enough, he felt naked without his claymore. Locked away in his chamber, his two-handed broadsword was as much a part of him as either hand. For the safety of the king and his family, they allowed no one to wear or carry a sword into the main gathering hall. Magnus's sword forged to accommodate his size, and even though custom designed, the enormous sword looked like little more than a young lad's wooden practice sword when Magnus held it. Needless to say, it was not a welcome sight strapped to his back. When he arrived the day before, he resigned himself to just carrying his dirks, of which he had at least eight on various parts of his body.

Arriving early the previous morning, Magnus spent all of the day and much of the evening in a passageway, standing, awaiting an audience with the king. This day came and went, just as the previous one had, with no indicator of when the king would meet with him. This only aggravated Magnus more as a representative from the Sinclair clan summoned rather than volunteered to attend court.

His Highland Surprise **BOOK 5 SNEAK PEEK**

Tavish Sinclair stood frozen in the Great Hall of his clan's keep as he listened to his father.

"Ye canna be serious!" He realized his voice was quiet as he spoke to Laird Liam Sinclair, but in his head, it was a roar. "I dinna need a wife. I dinna want a wife."

Tavish's body was so still he looked like a statue carved from marble, his expression like a death mask.

He canna mean it. I simply flirted one too many times with the elder man's daughter, Isabella. I will stay away and then this nonsense will pass.

"It isnae aboot Isabella or any of the local lasses ye ken so well. The king has decreed that I must make a match between our clans. Ye are the older of ma two unmarried sons. The duty falls to ye."

"But Magnus is already at court."

He recognized he sounded petulant, but Tavish Sinclair was a confirmed bachelor. He never intended to settle down with one woman. The Sinclair men, once their oath made, never were unfaithful to their wives. He refused to make that traditional vow, so instead he avoided marriage like it were a fire sweeping through hay.

"Aye, Magnus is at court. And taking far longer than expected. I worry something befell him. The king's message was rather cryptic on that front. I would have ye go to court and see that yer brother fares well, and while there, ye can meet the lass. Ye ken I will force none of ye into an unhappy marriage. I ask only that ye meet her. See if ye suit."

PIRATES OF THE ISLES

The Blond Devil of the Sea **BOOK 1 SNEAK PEEK**

Caragh lifted her torch into the air as she made her way down the precarious Cornish cliffside. She made out the hulking shape of a ship, but the dead of night made it impossible to see who was there. She and the fishermen of Bedruthan Steps weren't expecting any shipments that night. But her younger brother Eddie, who stood watch at the entrance to their hiding place, had spotted the ship and signaled up to the village watchman, who alerted Caragh.

As her boot slid along the dirt and sand, she cursed having to carry the torch and wished she could have sunlight to guide her. She knew these cliffs well, and it was for that reason it was better that she moved slowly than stop moving once and for all. Caragh feared the light from her torch would carry out to the boat. Despite her efforts to keep the flame small, the solitary light would be a beacon.

When Caragh came to the final twist in the path before the sand, she snuffed out her torch and started to run to the cave where the main source of the village's income lay in hiding. She heard movement along the trail above her head and knew the local fishermen would soon join her on the beach. These men, both young and old, were strong from days spent pulling in the full trawling nets and hoisting the larger catches onto their boats. However, these men weren't well-trained swordsmen, and the fear of pirate raids was ever-present. Caragh feared that was who the villagers would face that night.

The Dark Heart of the Sea **BOOK 2 SNEAK PEEK**

Ruairí MacNeil opened the door to the Three Merry Lads and tried not to curl his nose in disgust. The overpowering odor of too many bodies, stale beers, and burned food created a cloud of stench inside the tavern. Ruairí scanned the crowd as he stepped inside and immediately noticed that many members of his crew were already settled, a pint in one hand and a woman in the other. His ship, the *Lady Charity*, had docked an hour earlier. With their most recent bounty already stored in the nearby cave, Ruairí had granted them shore leave. He nodded his head once to his first mate, Kyle, who was the only sober one in the lot. Ruairí made another visual sweep of the room, checking whether there were any other sailors who might be less enthused to see him come ashore. When he was satisfied none of his rivals were waiting to stab him, he attempted to make his way to the bar. As he pushed through the standing-room-only main room, he noticed a tavern wench attempting to carry a tray of empty mugs to the bar. She was a sturdy sort, but short when compared to the mountainous Highlanders and Hebrideans who made up the patrons of the Lads. Ruairí couldn't help but smile as she tried to twist and shoulder her way past men who blocked her on purpose to give themselves more time to ogle her body.

It was rare that Ruairí felt mercy, sympathy, or compassion for anyone, let alone a woman, but there was an odd twinge in his heart as he watched her try to maintain her smile as she became more frustrated. The woman swatted away a hand that dared come too close to her modest neckline. That observation caused Ruairí to quirk a brow and inspect the woman. She had on a clean white blouse–a rarity in this tavern–and it fit loosely over her entire bust. It left much to the imagination, and Ruairí found his was alive and well. Her skirts reached her ankles instead of hiked up on either side like the other women who worked in the tavern. From what Ruairí could tell, she looked more like a farmer's wife than a tavern wench. She didn't fit in.

Ruairí's sense of compassion grew alongside his annoyance at not being able to make his way to the bar. He began to elbow men around him, and the crowd parted. Between his size and reputation, Ruairí MacNeil was a hard man to ignore. He grasped the top of the woman's hips and propelled her forward. She attempted to look over her shoulder, but she couldn't make out the man who was either her captor or her protector. When they made it to the bar, the woman set her tray down and spun around.

VIKING GLORY

Leif BOOK 1 SNEAK PEEK

Leif looked around his chambers within his father's longhouse and breathed a sigh of relief. He noticed the large fur rugs spread throughout the chamber. His two favorites placed strategically before the fire and the bedside he preferred. He looked at his shield that hung on the wall near the door in a symbolic position but waiting at the ready. The chests that held his clothes and some of his finer acquisitions from voyages near and far sat beside his bed and along the far wall. And in the center was his most favorite possession. His oversized bed was one of the few that could accommodate his long and broad frame. He shook his head at his longing to climb under the pile of furs and on the stuffed mattress that beckoned him. He took in the chair placed before the fire where he longed to sit now with a cup of warm mead. It had been two months since he slept in his own bed, and he looked forward to nothing more than pulling the furs over his head and sleeping until he could no longer ignore his hunger. Alas, he would not be crawling into his bed again for several more hours. A feast awaited him to celebrate his and his crew's return from their latest expedition to explore the isle of Britannia. He bathed and wore fresh clothes, so he had no excuse for lingering other than a bone weariness that set in during the last storm at sea. He was eager to spend time at home no matter how much he loved sailing. Their last expedition had been profitable with several raids of monasteries that yielded jewels and both silver and gold, but he was ready for respite.

Leif left his chambers and knocked on the door next to his. He heard movement on the other side, but it was only moments before his sister, Freya, opened her door. She, too, looked tired but clean. A few pieces of jewelry she confiscated from the holy houses that allegedly swore to a life of poverty and deprivation adorned her trim frame.

"That armband suits you well. It compliments your muscles," Leif smirked and dodged a strike from one of those muscular arms.

Only a year younger than he, his sister was a well-known and feared shield maiden. Her lithe form was strong and agile making her a ferocious and competent opponent to any man. Freya's beauty was stunning, but Leif had taken every opportunity since they were children to tease her about her unusual strength even among the female warriors.

"At least one of us inherited our father's prowess. Such a shame it wasn't you."

Freya **BOOK 2 SNEAK PEEK**

"Does he have nothing better to do than stare?" Freya huffed as she and Tyra left the training field.

Freya Ivarsdóttir was a renowned and much feared shieldmaiden and the daughter of a jarl. At twenty-four years old, she had already spent half of her life training and raiding with her Norse tribe.

Tyra looked back over her shoulder and scanned the field of battling Norsemen as they trained. As Freya's best friend, Tyra was used to Freya's sometimes brittle disposition, and she knew when her friend was hiding something. Nothing seemed out of the ordinary. The ongoing skirmishes against their neighbors and the general way of life in the northern Trondelag meant the men and women tasked with defending their tribes trained daily. Tyra watched as they swung axes, swords thrust, and spears hurled. She looked around at the many longhouses that created the perimeter of the homestead. Women stood outside doing laundry, one woman swept dust out her front door, and several people stood around engaged in easy conversation.

"I don't see anyone. Well, maybe a ghost from your past, but he's watched you for years."

"What? No. Wait, what do you mean he's watched me for years?"

"Ever since the two of you a few summers ago--- Well, you know. Skellig's had his eye on you, and I think you broke his heart. I believe he's hoping for more than just a reunion under the furs."

"Never."

"Then who could you have meant?" Tyra smirked before adding in a sing-song voice, "Erik?"

Tyra & Bjorn BOOK 3 SNEAK PEEK

10 years ago

Tyra extended her arm to Bjorn and jerked him from the ground where she had just knocked him onto his backside. She slid her foot under the hilt of his sword and kicked it until her hand wrapped around the handle. She handed it back to Bjorn with a smirk.

"Maybe one day you'll be able to keep up. Today isn't that day," Tyra goaded.

They had been sparing once more, and the result was typical. Tyra Vigosdóttir knocked Bjorn Jansson onto his arse time and again despite being two years younger, only coming to the middle of his chest, and being a woman. They had been sparring since they were children, and at seventeen, Bjorn resented Tyra, who was only fifteen, still being able to best him. He was a renowned warrior in his own right, but somehow Tyra read him better than he knew himself. She was always one, but usually three, moves ahead of him.

Before Bjorn could say thank you, she spun on her heels and marched away, her honey blonde braid swinging down her back. Bjorn grimaced as he recalled the loathing he had seen in her eyes as they fought. For the longest time, there had been a teasing glint as she bested him, but for the last three moons, it had been anger and disgust. He accepted that he deserved it, but it still stung.

He moved to the side of the training ring and stepped into the shadows as he took a long draw from the water skin. He watched as Tyra stood speaking to their friend Strian. Bjorn wanted to grimace at the sight of Strian and Tyra together, but he knew it was not his friend's fault. Bjorn's mind wandered to when they friendship ended three moons ago. Bjorn remembered as though the events were happening before his eyes. The early spring weather was unseasonably warm, and after training, Bjorn looked for Tyra as he usually did. He did not make a habit of talking to her or standing near her but having been in love with her since he was seven, he was used to being drawn to her. When he was unable to find her but spotted his cousins Leif and Freya, he wondered where Tyra disappeared to. She and Freya were best friends and rarely apart, so he made his way to his cousins as he looked around.

"You seem to be missing your other half," he grinned at Freya.

"Tyra was hot and wanted time to soak, so she went to the fjord."

"Alone?" Bjorn's heart began to race. Tyra was a force to be reckoned with when she was armed, but she would be vulnerable undressed and alone. "Why didn't you go with her?"

"She said she wanted some time to herself," Freya shrugged. "We aren't one person. We do things apart."

Bjorn grunted as he walked to the tree line then ran until he spotted the fjord to his left. He slowed his pace, cautious not to make his presence known in case someone did lurk within the trees watching Tyra. He drew his sword as he approached the shore. He scanned the area but could not hear nor see anyone else. His chest was tight with alternating pangs of fear and anger for Tyra's foolishness. He sheathed his sword and waded into the water. He had seen Tyra's blonde head sitting at the surface as the rest of her soaked. She stood and spun around a knife pointing at him when she heard his splashes.

Tyra's eyes opened wide as she took in Bjorn standing knee deep with a look of fury on his face. She had seen him angry countless times, usually directed at her for beating him, but this was far more intense than she had seen before.

Bjorn's mind screamed that his chest and cock would detonate simultaneously as both throbbed. He had been with more than one woman, and he had seen different body types over the years, but he had seen nothing as beautiful as the water nymph who stood before him. She was exquisite with long legs and slender hips. She had broad shoulders and muscles from years of training. Her breasts were not as large as usually drew him, but they would easily fill his hands. He forced his eyes from the thatch of dark hair that protected the place he most wanted to be at that moment.

"Bjorn?" her hushed tones barely carried to him.

Strian **VIKING GLORY BOOK 4**

Strian looked over his shoulder at the woman rowing just two benches behind him. Other Norsemen surrounded her, but she appeared out of place and alone. Despite trying to remain focused on navigating his ship towards the fjord just beyond his home, Strian Eindrideson failed to overcome the temptation to look back at Gressa time and again.

Gressa Jorgensdóttir refused to lift her gaze from the shoulder blades of the people seated in front of her. She followed the rhythm of the other rowers as her oar dipped and slid first through the water then in the air before returning to the water. She could feel Strian's eyes on her even though she had not looked up in hours. She refused. She refused to acknowledge him, and she refused to acknowledge her own feelings, or rather the ones he stirred in her. She forced her mind to focus on the motions needed to keep her oar synchronized with the other rowers. She would not allow herself to think about how her hands, blistered and raw, ached from rowing for hours after not having touched an oar in years. She would not think about how her stomach rumbled from refusing anything but the most meager amounts of food; one of the few rebellious acts available to her. She would not think about how once again fate forced an abrupt sacrifice of the life she had. She would not think about Strian. There was far more for her not to think about than what she was willing to entertain, but her attempts to force her mind away from the painful topics only made them linger in the forefront of her mind even more. Gressa caught herself before she shook her head.

Strian gave up all attempts at ignoring Gressa the second day aboard his ship. It was an exercise in futility to pretend she did not exist. He had never been able to ignore her, and ten years of separation had not changed that. Gressa stood out from the rest with her heart-shaped face, dark brown hair, and deep blue eyes with their almond shape, giving proof to her Sami heritage. None of her clothes resembled the ones he remembered. Gone were the conical rolled toes on her boots or the beading at the hems of her wrists and collar that she wore at home. The more subdued forest colors of a Welsh bowman replaced her Sami clothing. Her clothes had always made her stand out, first as a Sami and now as a Welshwoman. But Strian knew the clothes did not matter. His memories clutched to the images of Gressa when she was undressed. He snapped his eyes back to the water and slammed the door shut on those memories. They had haunted him ever since he last saw Gressa, and now they caused a painful knot to squeeze his heart.

"Captain, Tyra's given the signal that we are only five knots from the entrance to the fjord. We will be home soon." Strian nodded once to his first mate and followed the man to the stern where he took the rudder from one of his oarsmen.

Now that Strian was behind Gressa, it was easier for him to watch her. It was not so obvious when she was in his line of sight as he navigated the ice and sandbars. He had been sailing in and out of his homestead's natural harbor since he was a child. He could spare some of his attention and continue to watch Gressa. The linen shirt she wore stuck to her sweaty body, and he could see the muscles ripple through her back and shoulders as she continued to row. He watched her head twist slightly to the side as though she might look back at him. He knew she was aware he watched her, but he had caught her staring at him just as many times.

Strian guided his longboat into the harbor and docked beside Bjorn's and Tyra's boats. He avoided Freya because their falling out just before they left Scotland remained unresolved. Strian knew Freya felt guilty for their argument, and he did not enjoy being at odds with one of his oldest friends, but he would not overlook her high handedness as their leader or her unwillingness to hear why he wanted to remain in Scotland. Strian approached Gressa and waited until she noticed him. It was only a matter of a heartbeat before she looked up at him.

"Stay next to me," Strian whispered. When Gressa looked ready to object, Strian raised an eyebrow in warning. "It's been ten years."

Ivar's eyes swept across the battlefield as the hair on the back of his neck caused his sweat-covered skin to prickle. He took in the overcast skies—skies that did not match the scorching sun the Norse warriors had experienced during these last weeks in the Mediterranean. The darkened skies matched his current mood as he panted, trying to slow the adrenaline coursing through him after his last engagement with their Arab enemies. He had just slayed an enormous dark-skinned man whose guttural Arab language was still foreign to Ivar Sorenson's Norse ears. As Ivar looked into the dead man's vacant eyes, he watched a crow's reflection fly overhead. Odin's messengers Hunnin and Munnin brought a cheer from Ivar's fellow Norse warriors, who celebrated their victory with praise to their gods. But Ivar could not be less interested in prayer as he once again scanned the fallen bodies and those still on their feet, looking for a particular blonde head with a face that possessed the deepest cobalt-blue eyes he had ever seen. Ivar's stomach clenched as he searched for Lena Tormudsdóttir.

"Lena? Lena!" Ivar called out as his heart began to pound with fear unlike any he had experienced in the battle only moments earlier. "Lena!"

"Ivar?"

Ivar ran in the direction of the voice that he feared he would never hear again; it had never sounded sweeter. He wove through members of his clan and leaped over the bodies of fallen Arabs and Norsemen, pushing past a group of women to where Lena stood. Disregarding those around him, Ivar pulled Lena into his arms. After a brief glance to reassure himself that she was uninjured, he stroked her cheek and dove in for a searing kiss that brought conversations around them to an abrupt end.

Lena's toes curled within her boots. The feel of Ivar's body pressed against hers reminded her of their time spent coupling the night before. Her hands roamed over his back and shoulders as the tension eased with each of her caresses. The intensity of his kiss deepened as he groaned within her mouth, his tongue swirling and mating with hers, mimicking what they both longed to do with their bodies.

When they broke apart at last, their foreheads pressed together, Ivar smattered kisses on the tip of her nose as he cupped her jaw.

"You scared me," Ivar's hushed voice brushed warm air across Lena's face.

"You're scared of nothing, or so you told me," Lena brushed her lips against Ivar's.

"There is a first for everything. I couldn't find you."

"But you did. You're holding me now," Lena pressed another soft kiss to Ivar's mouth.

Ivar pulled back and swept Lena into his arms. He did not look back to see who snickered or tossed randy comments at his back, nor did he care that his father's commander, Magnus, was calling to him. Ivar carried Lena across the low grassy field to a copse of olive trees, cursing that their spindly branches would not give him the privacy that the fir trees in the Trondelag would offer. When they were a safe distance from the others, he placed Lena on her feet again and pulled her against him.

"Now I am holding you," Ivar's voice rumbled within his broad chest. "And I intend to hold you all through the night as I make love to you over and over until I am convinced you are safe and within my reach."

Made in the USA
Coppell, TX
14 January 2022